THE BOOK OF SIGHT

D0557391

BY

DEBORAH DUNLEVY

Copyright @2011 Deborah Dunlevy

Printed in the United States of America.

First Printing, 2013

Digital Edition ISBN: 978-0-9847624-2-2

Print Edition ISBN: 978-0-9847624-3-9

Madison House Publishing

www.madisonhousepublishing.com

Quantity sales. Special discounts are available on quantity purchases by corporations, associations, and others. For details, contact the publisher at the web-address above or call 317-797-9993.

www.TheBookOfSight.com

For Dad, who started me on this journey

For Mom, who always said I should do it

And for Nate, who has a way of making
dreams into reality

Contents

Chapter 1

An Echo of the Refrain

In a plain house on a dull street in a nondescript neighborhood in a sleepy town near the mountains lived an ordinary girl named Alex. Ironically, Alex, whose full name was Alexandra Jilian Hughes, was named for the famous Greek conqueror Alexander the Great. This was ironic because, while Alexander the Great was renowned for his brilliant strategic mind and charismatic leadership, Alex Hughes was not renowned for anything. She was, as far as she or anyone else could tell, a perfectly average teenage girl. Average grades, average talents, average pastimes. She even looked unremarkable: brown hair, green eyes and nothing in her features that would make her stand out from any other 14-year-old.

All in all, it was the most probable thing in the world that Alexandra Hughes would live a long and thoroughly uninteresting life.

So much for probability.

One unassuming morning, the first day of summer vacation, Alex woke up earlier than she wanted to. Apparently no one had informed her body that it could now sleep until noon. She stayed in bed for a little while, but she knew she wasn't going to drift off again, and since nothing is more depressing than being in bed only wishing you could sleep, she got up.

Downstairs in the kitchen, she poured herself a bowl of cereal and shook her head at the untouched plate of dinner sitting on the table. Apparently her dad had forgotten about eating again. She poured a second bowl of cereal and a glass of orange juice and headed out the back door, balancing both bowls in one hand. The studio door had fortunately been left unlatched, so she pushed it open with her foot.

"Hey, Dad, I brought you some breakfast."

He gave a little jump and looked up confusedly. "Is it breakfast time already?"

"Yeah...well, it's morning at least. It may be more like dinner time for you. Did you work all night?"

He had already turned back to his drawing table. "Hmm? Oh...no, I slept on the couch out here for a few hours...there...sorry, I just wanted to finish that frame." He took the bowl of cereal. "Thanks, sweetie. What would I be without you?"

"Pretty hungry, probably. I noticed you never touched your dinner."

"Oh, yeah,' he said, as if just now realizing it. "I'm sorry. You worked hard on that. I just got on a roll and, you know, the time got away from me. I'm really close to finishing this one."

"It's okay," laughed Alex. "I didn't spend too much time on it." She didn't bother telling him that it was only a frozen TV dinner. She knew better than to waste much effort on meals when her dad was trying to finish a project. "You can make it up to me by eating your cereal, so I know you'll at least have one meal today."

They crunched in companionable silence for a few minutes.

"So what are you up to today?" he asked after the last spoonful.

"I don't know. Probably not much."

"Oh, hey, that's right. This is your summer break now."

"Yeah."

"Well, I'm sure there's a huge pile of dishes in there and the house is probably a mess, but don't you start cleaning today. This is your vacation. Do something fun. With any luck, I'll be done with this one in another day or two and then I'll take care of the house."

"You're that close?" asked Alex, looking over his shoulder at the pages of comic book pictures spread out on the table. "Can I see what you have so far?"

"Sure, most of them are in that stack right there. Help yourself."

She could tell from his voice that his mind had already turned back to his work. Alex cleared a spot on the couch and started in on the latest edition of *The Mist*, the moderately successful comic book her dad wrote and illustrated. She'd always loved reading her dad's work. His main character, a normal father and husband who gained the ability to turn himself into a vapor after an accident at a nuclear plant, had the perfect comeback and the perfect homemade weapon for every situation.

Reaching the end with a chuckle, she stretched and stood up, beginning to gather up the assortment of coffee cups and plates of half eaten food.

Her dad glanced up for a moment. "Promise me you won't spend the day working. I mean it, Magna."

Alex smiled. Alexandra Magna had been his pet name for her as long as she could remember, a reference to her namesake.

"I promise," said Alex, but he was already back to his drawing, and she wasn't sure if he heard her or not.

Adding the dishes to the precarious stack in the sink, Alex began to weigh her options for the day. There weren't too many. Dunmore wasn't exactly a great metropolis. The only real entertainment available to a 14-year-old was the dollar theater, and she'd already seen the movie that was showing there. Darcy, her best friend and the only person she would normally call, was leaving that afternoon for California, where she was spending the summer with her dad. She'd read every book in the house at least five times, and there wouldn't be anything on TV but cartoons at this time of day. Alex looked around at the crazy mess and began to wish she hadn't just promised not to the clean the house. She hoped this wasn't what the whole summer was going to be like.

There was a knock on the door.

On the porch was a rather unkempt looking man, a total stranger, and as contradictory as he was strange. The shiny leather satchel he carried stood out against his worn jeans and threadbare corduroy coat. His face was too weather-beaten for someone so obviously young, and though he had the tousled and dirty hair of a fierce lion, his brown eyes were warm and his look was kind.

Most people might have found him an alarming sight, but Alex was not fazed at all. She figured he was one of Dad's illustrator friends. The knock gave them away, when any normal person would have used the doorbell. They didn't come to the house too often, but they were usually too lost in their own worlds to notice the little button by the door. One time one of them had showed up in a snowstorm wearing only shorts and a t-shirt. He hadn't even seemed to feel the cold. This one fit the bill exactly.

"Can I help you?" she asked.

"Are you Alex Hughes?" asked the man.

"Yes."

"I have a package for you."

That did take Alex by surprise. "For me?"

He held up a smallish rectangular package, wrapped in plain brown paper. Sure enough, there was her name printed neatly on the front. She started to reach for it, and then stopped.

"Are you a UPS guy?" He didn't look like a UPS guy.

"No, I'm... with a private delivery service." Noticing that she still hesitated, he smiled, a bright flash that changed his whole appearance. "Don't worry, it won't explode. It's a book."

Alex took the package. It was obvious from the feel that it was, in fact, a book, and a heavy one at that. She turned it over. There was no return address. "Do you know who it's from?"

"It should say inside."

"Do I need to sign or anything?"

"No, that's not necessary," the man smiled again. "Have a nice day...and enjoy your book."

Closing the door, Alex ripped off the brown wrapper and stared with surprise at the book in her hand. It was thick and appeared to be incredibly old. The red leather cover was faded and water-stained, and the pages were slightly yellow.

Who would send her an antique book? She checked the wrapper for a note, but there was none. She turned the book over and checked the inside cover. No writing. No indication at all of who it was from.

Sinking into the armchair in the living room, she started to read. And then she stopped.

It was complete nonsense. The words literally did not make sense, weren't even words. If it was another language, it was one she couldn't remotely recognize. This line, now: "Humtel slarmed alto the viristren." What on earth was that? It must have been sent to her by mistake. Alex tossed the book on the table.

She picked it up again. After all, the man had known her name. She carefully searched the wrapper again. Nothing. She flipped through the pages. Nothing but nonsense, or some mystery language, all the way through. It had to be a mistake.

But somehow she couldn't just put it aside. It was a mystery. There must be something she was missing. Anyway, what else was she going to do with her morning? She flipped back to the first page and tried again to read.

And that was it. It really was the strangest thing. She *could* understand it. Not that the words made any more sense, but as she read them, images formed themselves in her mind. It was a story...the most beautiful story Alex had ever read. As it unfolded before her inner eye, she forgot all about the strange nonsense words and got lost in another world...

The king hurries down the stone steps, fear perched like a bird of prey with its claws imbedded in his heart...every heartbeat is an echo of the refrain, the jewel, the jewel, the jewel, the jewel, he must protect the jewel...a flash of yellow light, a triumphant face, a sinking despair...

a boy, too young and too skinny...everything he sees impresses the boy more and more with his own awkwardness and inadequacy...the king slumps next to the fountain, gray and deflated, like a once proud flag hanging limp and dull, muttering over and over, it is gone, all is lost, it is gone, all is lost...

a pity so deep it touches subterranean levels of courage is born in the boy's heart, he must, he will find a way to ease the king's suffering...

a whisper, so fragile it might be leaves on the wind, the jewel, the jewel, the heart of the kingdom, it is lost, how can it be restored? it cannot, it cannot...

it can, it must, we will, we can...

what light flickers in the king's eyes...the prophecy rings out (where did the strength come from for such clear tones?) while the circle remains unbroken none shall enter there...gendel sea...gendel sea...

a thrill of recognition as three young men enter the garden in search of their brother...

Alex came to herself with a gasp. Her heart was pounding in time with the boy's, the words of the prophecy rang in her ears, and the smell of the fading garden was all around her. The shock of finding herself sitting in her own living room left her dazed for a moment. Her stomach growled as if it had been hours since she ate breakfast, but the pull of the book was much stronger than the pull of hunger.

...a journey of brothers begun in blazing expectation covered with humble cloaks...

a kingdom undone, a people in desolation...pigs eating in the hall of a once beautiful home...a child cradling her mother's head, dry-eyed and mute with despair...a putrid stream, a foul stench, dry dust on the tongue...a man with a gap-toothed smile selling rotten fruit...

high spirits have long flown, slowly replaced by a steely resolve...

the imposing ramparts of the black castle loom above, dwarfing the four brothers and shrinking their hearts...cold, cold, icy claws penetrating deep into the bones...the stone passage opens like a dark hungry mouth...

a slender bridge over a yawning chasm...impossible, impassible, a breathtaking, hollow stomach frozenness...inch by inch, certainty of death foremost in his mind, not daring to breath...

a brother's hand, strong and reassuring, steady, steady...

the rush of relief swallowed up in cold...cold, cold, icy breath penetrates everything...mind numb, limbs wooden, stumbling, stumbling...huddled together for warmth, hope wanes...

a small light, purple and distant and alive...

the jewel! the jewel!...the solid warmth in his hand radiates throughout his body...the brothers' faces glow, each reflecting the others' radiance...

hurrying along, stumbling again, stumbling but this time with eager joy...relief, freedom, out the black arch and into the free air, gasping, laughing, running...

And on it went, the images building toward a conclusion that left Alex breathless. When at last it released her, she looked up, her mind reeling, and noticed that it was already getting dark. Had she been reading all day? But she'd only read...could it just have been five pages?! Normally she was a quick reader. On the other hand, she had never read anything like this before. It was.... She had no idea how to describe it. It was not like a story at all, but more like

11

living in another world. She could not only see but feel and smell and taste what was going on around her. The people in the book were more real than any person she'd ever met in her life.

She knew she couldn't read any more right now. Her mind felt full to bursting. Still, it was with regret that she set the book down.

Outwardly, Alex passed the rest of the evening as normal. She fixed herself some dinner and took some out to her dad. He didn't even look up this time, so she left the food on his table. Back inside, she ate alone, took a shower and brushed her teeth. But the whole time, she felt like she was sleep walking. She kept reliving the scenes of the story in her head over and over.

That night as she went to bed, she saw the trees outside her window whispering to each other.

Chapter 2

A Flash of Yellow Light

A rational person will have no problem explaining away whispering trees as nothing more than wind in the branches combined with an overactive imagination. This is only one of the many shortcomings of rational people.

In any case, the whispering was only the beginning for Alex. She awoke from a night of vivid dreams to a day of blazing sunshine. Light was streaming through the window and creating brilliant leafy patterns on the wall opposite her bed. Something about it gave Alex a deep feeling of satisfaction. For several minutes she just lay there and appreciated the intricate design. Then she rolled herself out of bed.

As soon as she opened her bedroom door, she was greeted by the unmistakable smell of cooking bacon. This, together with the clattering and banging issuing from the kitchen, was evidence that her dad had, as promised, finished his latest issue.

The completion of a project always meant a few days of undivided attention from her dad and lots of frenzied activity on his part. It was as if he was determined to fit a month's worth of cooking, cleaning, talking, and playing into three days. For as long as she could remember she had looked forward to these times, which with characteristic creativity she had dubbed "dad days."

Today was a classic dad day. When Alex entered the kitchen, not only was there breakfast on the table but the dishes were washed, a lunch was packed in the cooler, and the fishing poles were propped against the back door. In less than an hour, she and her dad were in the truck headed toward Fox Creek.

Looking out the window as they bumped along, Alex was stunned by the beauty of the day. The sky was such a vibrant blue it took her breath away, and the sun was glowing with an intensity she could not find words for. It wasn't that it was bright or blinding, but almost more alive. It warmed her skin like a physical touch and seemed to infuse everything in sight with a particular brilliance. The pavement ahead of them sparkled, the mountain peaks in the distance glittered, and the trees stretched out to embrace the life-giving warmth.

The trees...suddenly Alex remembered the whispering from last night and the dreams. In the rush of the last hour she had almost forgotten the mysterious book. Now it all came flooding back. The sweetness of the story seemed to fit with the loveliness of the day.

"We're here, Magna."

Alex came back to the present with a start. She hadn't even noticed that they had stopped.

Her dad chuckled. "You okay? Get lost in your thoughts?"

"Yeah, I was just... It's a beautiful day."

"Sure is." He jumped out of the car, grinning. "Perfect for sitting by a creek and not catching any fish. It feels great to be outside again."

Collecting all the gear, he led the way down to the creek. Alex followed, soaking in the beauty all around her. The sun was starting to hurt her eyes, but she still couldn't get enough of looking at everything. The grass even...was there a name for that shimmering shade of green?

All morning as she sat on the bank, chatting with her dad and, true to his prediction, not catching any fish, Alex could not stop feeling overwhelmed by the colors and the brightness around her. She stared around so much she could feel a headache coming on and finally lay back against a log and closed her eyes to rest them.

15

The Book of Sight

Even through her eyelids she could see the sunlight, muted and pastel. It was lovely, but it didn't help the headache any. She leaned over and dipped her hands in the water and pressed them against her face.

She must have been making a pained face because her dad looked concerned and asked, "You alright, baby? Getting too hot?"

"No, I'm fine, Dad. It's just the sun getting to my eyes a little."

"You want to borrow my sunglasses?"

"Sure. Thanks."

She slid the sunglasses on, and the change was so abrupt it was startling. Everything was incredibly dark. It felt like being blind. A strange sense of panic swept over her, and she pulled the glasses off. The sunlight exploded around her again causing her to squint. Still, she didn't put the glasses back on.

Instead, she said, "I think I'm going to go sit in the shade for a little bit, Dad."

"Hey, we can just pack up and head home, if you're ready, Magna."

"Yeah, that might be good. My head is hurting a little."

"No problem. I'll get the poles. You pack up the rest of the lunch."

16

It was then, when Alex turned to fold up the picnic blanket, that she saw it. Or rather, saw *him*. Right at the edge of the trees, standing among a clump of wildflowers in the grass, was a tiny man, less than a foot tall. Alex froze. She didn't take her eyes off the little man. He was looking right back at her, not moving. She noticed that he was wearing all green, the same green as the grass, and had on a hat of just the same purple as the flowers. In fact, he blended in so perfectly that she wouldn't have seen him at all if it hadn't been for his eyes. They were a light gold and gleamed in the reflected light from the creek.

"Ready?"

Alex jumped at her dad's hand on her shoulder. She looked back toward the little man, but there was nothing. Just a clump of flowers. She shook herself. This headache was obviously worse than she thought. Alex continued folding up the blanket and put it in the basket with the leftover food.

When she straightened up, there he was again, in another clump of flowers closer to the creek this time.

"Dad, look at that!" She grabbed his arm and pointed.

"At what? The flowers?"

"In the flowers…that little guy!"

"What little guy?"

She turned to him in disbelief. It was so close! How could he not see him? He was looking right where she was pointing. She turned back. The little man was gone again. Did she just imagine that? She narrowed her eyes and scanned the bank but couldn't see anything. Suddenly her head was throbbing.

"I don't see anyone, honey," her dad was watching her closely. "Are you okay? That headache getting worse?"

"Yeah, I don't feel very good. I thought I saw... Must have just been my eyes playing tricks on me."

"Let's get you home, baby."

At home, Alex lay on the couch in the cool, dark family room. She couldn't sleep, but it felt good to have her eyes closed. Without meaning to, she found herself thinking about the little man she thought she saw...and the unnatural brightness of the day...and the whispering trees last night...and the dreams about the wonderful story. It all led back to the strange book. She sat up.

The book was next to her bed upstairs. Alex picked it up and ran her hand over the cover. It was old and stained like she remembered, but now she noticed that the faded red leather was actually covered front and back with a lightly etched pattern, all swirls and curls, gold on the red background. She opened it again. On the first page where a title would normally be, there was just one word: SEE. She must have skipped over it last night.

Turning again to the story she had read the night before she was quickly lost again in the tale that felt more than ever like it was happening all around her.

...an invisible hand halts the brothers, pain floods their limbs... the white face, the yellow eyes, the low sweet voice, the sorcerer!...

hand in hand and back, the brothers encircle the jewel... the prophecy rings in their ears, 'while the circle remains unbroken none shall enter there'...

a blue ring of fire springs up around the brothers, trapped!...and then the tempting...money, lands, fame, love, all shall go to the one who brings out the jewel...

who are these brothers anyway?...remember when? the stolen toy, the father's love, the fight that came to blows, the girl with the golden braids...hearts full of confusion, the brothers look away, but do not let go...those words, those insidious words, they won't leave their heads, remember, remember, you never received what you deserved, now is your time, see, he cannot even look you in the eye...

the grip begins to weaken...

then the sweet voice falters, stops, the brothers look up, the king! the king!...

white-faced, weakened, but with sword raised, the king descends upon the sorcerer, calling aloud the words of the prophecy...gendel sea! gendel sea!...

the brothers' heads are cleared, their hearts turn to each other, hands grasp tightly, a song of joy shared on all tongues...

then a flash of light, the king falls, a ruby dagger in his chest...impossible! how can he be lost?!...

the brothers' song falters, but the jewel's light grows, a blazing royal light fills them as if from within, the song is renewed, but the ring of fire grows in response...

the king's dying breath, a spell of power, unheard as the song rings joyfully out...

brothers' feet joining with the soil, brothers' hands entwining, brothers grow in strength and solidity...

a cry of recognition and rage escapes the sorcerer, his hurled spells to no avail...

where once had been a circle of brothers now stands a circle of trees, solidly planted, the jewel buried deep in the protected center...

the sorcerer flees as the healing radiates from the circle...a kingdom renewed, a people restored, the wind plays a joyful song in the branches of the brothers' circle...

gendel sea...gendel sea...

This time when it came to an end Alex felt a sudden and aching sense of loss. She wanted to read more. She turned the page to start the next chapter, but it was all nonsense, and no matter how many times she reread it and tried to figure it out, it remained impenetrable.

In frustration, Alex dropped the book and climbed into bed, and the headache which had been forgotten in the delight of the story pounded back and kept her tossing and turning all night.

* * * * *

The next three days were spent mainly with her dad. True to form, he took her out for ice cream, beat her at Monopoly, and rented movies every night.

Alex continued to be plagued by headaches which were especially bad if she spent much time outside, but each day the headache was less intense. She also continued to see strange things, though nothing as strange as the tiny man. Twice she saw a rock move on its own power; the pond in the park reflected everything around it in colors that were completely different from the colors of the actual objects; and once she had seen a dark shadow when there was nothing to cast a shadow. That last one had given her a very unpleasant shiver.

It wasn't just new things, either. She began to notice unexpected details about places that she had thought she knew very well. For example, the elaborately carved façade on the old Stokes mansion, which she had always been fascinated with, suddenly had sculptures on it that she could not remember having seen before. And was that statue on the courthouse lawn actually smirking?

Every night before bed, Alex found herself drawn to the book to read and reread the beautiful story. It continued to amaze and delight her. Each new reading evoked some new emotion. Sometimes she felt overwhelmed by sadness, other times a bubble of laughter came to her lips; at times she was bursting with pride and suppressed excitement, at others she felt a burning shame.

On the fourth day, Alex woke up to find that her dad had retreated to his studio once more. She automatically picked up the book to begin reading again, but today it felt flat. Idly turning the pages, her eyes were drawn to the ending. She just had to close her eyes and she could see in her mind exactly what the trees looked like, hear the soft breeze in the branches, smell the pungent earthy scent. Suddenly her eyes flew open. She knew why that place felt so familiar. And she knew what she was going to do today.

* * * * *

The trees were exactly as Alex had remembered them. Just at the edge of town, behind the Super-Mart, was an empty field. And at the far side of that field eight slender aspen trees formed a perfect circle.

Alex paused, surprised by a sudden rush of joy. These were the trees from the story.

True, in some part of her mind, she knew that her brain had just supplied the image of these trees, which she had seen hundreds of times, when the book had mentioned a circle of trees. But she couldn't shake the feeling that the story had been about *these* trees.

And anyway, the book hadn't said anything about a circle of trees. It had only said a bunch of nonsense words that made her think of a circle of trees. The whole thing made no sense, but Alex didn't care. She was excited about her discovery.

Alex walked across the field toward the circle with a prickly sense of anticipation. What was she going to find in the circle? She had felt, still felt, that she had to come here. That this was the next step. The next step of what, she had no idea.

Arriving at the circle, Alex put a hand on the smooth white trunk of the nearest tree. She felt an almost electric shock at the sensation of life pulsing under her hand.

She entered the circle.

And there was just more grass. Crisp, vital, glowing grass, but nothing else, no strange sights, no funny clues. True, the trees stood straight and beautiful, reminding her strongly of a circle of guards, giving the whole circle of feeling of safety. But it wasn't what she had expected.

She walked around the circle, brushing each tree with her hand. And then she noticed it. Very small, carved into the base of the largest tree, a circle within a circle within a circle, each touching at one side. Heart beating, Alex bent down to examine it more closely when a voice behind her made her jump.

"So you read it, too?"

Chapter 3

Cry of Recognition

Alex whirled around.

Standing there with a very curious look on his face was a boy about her age. He was just slightly shorter than she, with sandy hair and glasses. She'd never seen him before.

"I'm Adam Cleary," he said, sticking out his hand.

"Um, Alex."

"I don't think I've seen you around. Jefferson Middle School?" When she nodded, he said, "I go to Lewis. Or, went to, I guess. I'll be in high school next year."

"Me too."

"Cool." He could barely contain himself as he rushed on. "So did you? Read it, I mean?" Without waiting for an answer, he pulled out of his backpack a very familiar faded red book.

Alex felt the tingle again. "You have the same book!"

"I knew it!" Adam was triumphant. "And when you saw this place, you recognized it from the story?"

"Yeah, sort of. I mean, I've seen it a thousand times, and when I read the story I thought of it."

"Crazy. I'd never been here before, but I found it yesterday and it was so much like the story that I wanted to come back today." He was still looking at her curiously. "So, where did you get the book?"

"A guy just came to my house and delivered it. My name was on the package, but it didn't say who it was from."

"No way." Adam shook his head. "That's what happened to me, too. That's so weird. I wonder who sent them? It couldn't have been anyone who knows both of us, could it? I mean, we've never even seen each other, but we both got the same book sent to us in the same way? It's freaky, right?"

"Yeah."

"I wish I had talked to that guy some more," he continued. "My mom was rushing me out the door when he came. He just asked me if I was Adam Cleary, I said yes, he handed me the package, and then she was pushing me into the car. She was late for a showing or something. My mom's a realtor, and she's always rushing off somewhere. But I really wish I'd had a minute to ask him some questions. My mom was muttering all the way in the car about how scruffy that UPS man looked and how no one is professional anymore, but somehow I don't think he worked for UPS, you know? Did he say anything to you?"

"Not really. He said something about a private delivery service. I probably should have asked him more, but I figured there would be a note inside saying who it was from. I mean, it's not like I knew the book was going to be...well..." Alex didn't really know how to finish. She half turned away, and there was an uncomfortable silence.

Finally Adam said, "So, um...did you have a hard time reading it at first?"

"Yeah," Alex answered. "I mean, it's just nonsense words, isn't it? But once I started trying to really read it, it just sort of started to make sense. It was like I couldn't necessarily understand the words any better, but I could see the story in my head as I was reading."

29

Adam looked thoughtful. "Weird. It was different for me. At first, no matter what I did, I couldn't understand anything. I thought maybe it was in another language, but it didn't sound like any language I'd ever heard of. It was like a puzzle or something. It made me think of that poem *Jabberwocky*, you know, the one with all the made up words but it still makes sense. Only this was even worse. At first I was annoyed, but then it got kind of fun to piece it together. And then once I got going it got easier and easier to understand it. You know what I mean? I couldn't really translate the words or anything, but I could get the meaning from the context." He broke off, looking a little embarrassed. "Anyway. We both read it. It's amazing, isn't it?"

"The best thing I've ever read," said Alex. "I've probably read it ten times this week. But only the first story. Even though that one makes sense, I can't understand any of the other ones at all."

"Me either," said Adam, shaking his head in disbelief. "If it's a code, it's a different one for each chapter. Man, this is so weird. I keep saying that. But it is."

There was another pause.

"So what do you think the book *is*?" Adam burst out.

"I don't know." Alex tried to put her thoughts into words. "I'm not sure where it comes from or anything. But I think I like it." She hesitated, but then took the plunge, "And I think it does something to you, if you know what I mean."

"Yeah, I do. It's like ever since I read it... well... have you seen anything weird lately?"

Alex nodded, feeling that little tingle on her spine again. "You, too?"

"Yeah."

He was looking at her as if waiting for her to go on, so she said, "I've seen some things move that shouldn't move. And the trees were sort of whispering together." She glanced at Adam, but he didn't seem to think she was crazy. Instead he was nodding along. Taking heart, she added, "And down by the creek the other day, I think I saw a little, sort of man thing really small among the flowers."

Adam's eyes widened, but with excitement not disbelief. "Wow, that's amazing. I've seen some stuff moving around, too. Some flowers in my neighbor's yard. And the tree thing, too. And I've seen some pictures in the clouds. And not just the imaginary kind that you look for when you're a kid, but like real pictures, all lined up like they're telling a story or

31

something." It was his turn to look at her hesitantly.

Alex was not having any trouble believing him. "I haven't noticed that, but it does sort of fit."

"And today is the first day since I read the book that I haven't had a headache," Adam said.

Alex felt her heart thumping. "Me, too. It's like the sun was too bright all of a sudden. But it makes everything so beautiful, like you just want to keep looking and looking even though it hurts your eyes."

"I know what you mean," said Adam. "Yesterday I spent half an hour just watching the light sparkling through water from the sprinkler in my backyard. It was like little rainbows flying everywhere. I know. It sounds lame."

"No, it doesn't." Alex smiled. "It sounds beautiful. You'll have to show me sometime."

As soon as she said it, Alex felt weird about it. It was like the question was just hanging out there: So what now?

It is one thing to have read a book and discovered all sorts of things exist that you didn't know existed. It is another thing (quite a satisfying thing) to discover someone else who had the same experience, so you know you aren't crazy. But none of that tells you why it is happening or what you are supposed to do now that you realize it is happening.

Adam broke into Alex's thoughts. "So do you think that other people have read the book and are seeing things, too?"

Alex considered. Ever since she got the book, it seemed like one thing just naturally led to another, ending in her meeting Adam. Meeting just one person who knew about the book was coincidence enough. It was hard to imagine more. Of course, all of this was hard to imagine.

Adam went on, "I'm guessing so. I mean, it only makes sense that if two of us got it there are probably more. I just wish we could find the others."

Alex spoke without thinking. "They'll probably come here, won't they? This is the meeting place."

"The meeting place? How do you know that?"

"I don't know," Alex was as surprised as he was. "I guess it's just...the circle of trees is in the story, and the circle symbol is carved on this tree. And like you said, we both read the book and then came here. It just seems right."

Adam was nodding. "A meeting place...of course. I didn't really think of it that way; I was just so excited to find some place that was like the story. But we were both drawn here, weren't we? Anyone else who read the story would be bound to find this place, too."

"So I guess we'll meet any others right here."

"Yeah. But...are we just going to hang out here all day waiting for them to come? It seems like we should be doing something...trying to figure all this out. How about if we just check back here every once in a while and in the mean time go and check out the things that each of us has seen since we read the book? I mean, I'd like to get a look at that little man you were talking about." His enthusiastic look was back.

"I don't even know if he was real," cautioned Alex. "My head was hurting pretty bad that day."

Adam grinned. "There's only one way to find out."

Chapter 4

The Wind Plays a Joyful Song

Normally, Alex could never think of much to say to people when she first met them, but pedaling along together on their bikes made conversation easier.

Adam was talkative, and their shared experiences with the strange book gave them plenty to talk about. By the time they arrived at the creek, Alex felt like she'd known Adam for years.

The fishing spot looked exactly as it had a few days ago. The crispness and lush colors were still awe-inspiring, but Alex's eyes seemed to be getting used to the brilliant sunlight. She pointed out to Adam the two places where she had noticed the little man.

At the moment, there was nothing. The two of them looked around for a while without seeing anything. Finally, Alex sat down on a fallen log and gazed off toward the tree line while Adam wandered a little way down the creek still looking from side to side as if searching for clues.

Alex was feeling a bit foolish. Maybe she hadn't really seen anything at all. It was a pretty big leap from bright colors and whispering trees to tiny men that live in the forest. But just as she was about to call out that they should head back, she saw a pair of eyes peeking out of a tangle of vines hanging from the nearest trees. She gave a little cry. Adam immediately looked up and came running back to her.

"Did you see something?"

Alex just pointed, afraid to blink or move her head.

"Oh, my...," Adam breathed, and Alex felt a rush of adrenalin. He could see it, too!

They both stared at the eyes for a few moments, hardly breathing. Then a tiny figure stepped gracefully from the trees and stood in plain sight, smiling at the two of them. This was not the same one that Alex had seen before. That had been a man, but this was clearly a little woman. She, too, was about 10 inches tall, but she had clear, deep green eyes and a tangle of dark brown hair woven with green vines. She was dressed all in shades of brown.

Alex stood up and walked a couple of steps forward. "He-Hello?" she said hesitantly.

"Hello!" answered the little woman in a voice that was high-pitched and sweet, but surprisingly strong for such a small person. "You returned. And you have brought another with you."

"Um, yes," answered Alex. "You were here the other day? You remember me?"

"I was not here myself," replied the tiny stranger. "That was Florin. But of course he could not forget you. You saw him!" She uttered these last words as if they were an astonishing announcement.

"I guess that doesn't happen very often."

"None of us has been seen by a human in many generations of my people. Though many humans come here, they never really look at anything. I have often been sitting right here when a man passed within inches of me and never noticed my presence. We had begun to think that the tales of humans with eyes that see were only myths. And then four days ago Florin came back to the home with news of a young human girl who had looked right into his eyes and seen him. A few laughed, but most of us decided to post a watch to see if you would return. And now you have. And you are not alone." She nodded her head toward Adam, still standing silent and amazed.

37

"Yes," said Alex, realizing that an introduction was expected. "This is Adam...he read the...I mean, he can see you, too. And I'm Alex."

"Adam, Alex," repeated the little woman slowly and carefully, "it is a great pleasure to meet you. I am Terra."

Now Adam stepped forward. "So there are a lot of you living in these woods?"

"I do not know what would be a lot. We are enough. The four families are thriving and the wood is filled with our enjoyment. I am sure that the Grandparents know the exact number of us, but I have never asked."

"And what *are* you?" asked Adam.

Alex wondered if Terra would be offended by the question, but she didn't seem to mind at all.

"We are the Gylf. Our families have lived in these woods as far back as the traditions remember. This is the first time anyone from our families has talked to a human in the memory of even our oldest Grandfather. But we are very glad to welcome you. You have sight. We always welcome any creature with sight."

Adam and Alex traded a look, but before they could say anything, Terra was beckoning them into the forest.

"Come, I will take you to our home. My cousins will be so happy to meet you."

There was nothing to do but follow her.

If you ever find yourself following a ten-inch-tall woman through a fairly dense forest, you will understand how difficult Alex and Adam found it. Terra slipped between trees and through tangles of vines where it was impossible for them to follow. Sometimes they couldn't even see where she had gone until she reappeared somewhere further along and called to them. She was very patient, however, and obviously bright because before long she realized that her usual path was not suitable for people six times her size and found her way to a sort of animal trail that made following somewhat easier.

For Alex, the whole experience had the surreal quality of a dream, the sort of dream in which you find yourself doing things that you know are impossible but it feels perfectly natural to you, and you don't notice anything abnormal until you wake up. The only difference was that this time there was no waking up. Instead, there was a sense of anticipation, not knowing what was coming next but being certain that it would be stranger and more wonderful than anything that had happened so far.

Suddenly, Terra stopped. They were in a small clearing where a roughly flat, mossy rock was surrounded by wildflowers. The trees leaned in ever so slightly so that, though there was space

39

among the trunks, overhead there was a thick roof of branches.

"Welcome to our home," said Terra.

Alex looked around in surprise. She wasn't sure what she had expected, but at the moment she didn't see anything at all. Where were all the other Gylf, Terra's cousins?

She heard Adam whisper, "Whoa." And as she stood, looking around in confusion, things began to change. It was like that ugly 3D picture at her Uncle Gabe's house; one minute it was just a bunch of lines and the next minute there was a picture. As if her eyes were suddenly coming into focus, she saw that there were faces looking out from the trees all around her and from the flowers in front of her. There must have been thirty Gylf standing around the clearing; there were even a couple sitting on top of the rock.

Then Alex realized why she hadn't seen them at first. Each one was wearing clothing that blended in perfectly with their surroundings. Those among the tree trunks wore rough brown clothing very like Terra's. Those in the flowers were wearing the green pants and flowered hats that she had noticed on the little man, Florin, the first day. And those on the rock wore clothing of wrinkled gray mottled with mossy green. It was such perfect camouflage that only their faces stood out.

Now they were all emerging into the clearing. The ones on the rock stood up and smiled. As they approached, Alex could see that though they were all roughly the same height as Terra and had the same fine features and large eyes, they did not all look alike. Alex saw hair ranging from short bristly grey to almost transparent wispy blonde to long dark tangles. There were eyes as deep and green as forest pools and eyes bright and sparkling blue and eyes as grey as slates. Some of the Gylf seemed young and had smooth care-free faces and others were old and leaned on knobbly wooden sticks.

One of these, an old man who moved slowly, though his long hair was still thick and dark, looked up at Adam and Alex and extended a hand in greeting. "Welcome, humans. You are the first of your kind to visit our home. We are pleased to meet the seeing ones that our traditions speak of."

There was much excited murmuring at this. All the Gylf were looking in wonder at the kids. Alex felt self-conscious with all the staring, but there was nothing malicious in it. On the contrary, the Gylf all seemed very happy with this unexpected encounter.

"Thank you," said Adam. "It's really great to meet you, too. You may have stories of us, but we've never even heard of you. This incredible."

41

"Yes," said the old man. "Your people are known for blindness. But we should be introduced." He looked meaningfully at Terra.

She stepped forward at once. "Yes, Grandfather, this is Alex. She is the one who saw Florin. And this is Adam who came with her today to find us. Alex, Adam, this is my grandfather, Terfol. And," indicating a very old woman with long fair hair in braids down her back, "Celana, one of our grandmothers."

The old woman looked up with a very young twinkle in her blue eyes and a beautiful smile that lit up her face. "Welcome, young ones. The other grandfathers and grandmothers are in the forest today," she said sweetly. "We did not, of course, know that you would be coming, but they will be pleased to be introduced to you in due time. And now, your coming is cause for celebration!"

She clapped her hands, and all the Gylf laughed and began to clap with her. Their clapping turned quickly into a rhythmic beat, and some began to stomp their feet. A few of the younger Gylf began to dance and soon all but the two grandparents were whirling and stamping and laughing in a circle around Adam and Alex. The joy in the little clearing was like a fountain, and Alex felt it flow into her and well up in a bubble of laughter. Beaming, she turned to look at Adam who was clapping and stamping along

42

with the rest. He caught her eye, and they both grinned.

The tempo around them increased. The Gylf were swinging and spinning faster and faster until some lost their footing and tumbled into a heap or collapsed, breathless and laughing outside the circle. Those who were still dancing called jokingly to them, but once someone had sat down, he did not join the dance again. Instead each one clapped along and increased the pace more and more until only a few were left on their feet. Finally, one of these last dancers tripped and all the others stumbled over her and came crashing down together. Obviously this was a well-established game because all the Gylf laughed at this ending and jumped to their feet to help untangle the winners.

After such an exuberant welcome, Alex and Adam could not help but feel perfectly at home. They sat in the clearing and talked with Terfol and Celana while the younger Gylf prepared food and carried out their normal tasks. Alex loved watching them; they moved quickly without ever seeming to hurry and frequently exchanged comfortable jokes.

Adam was much more interested in talking with Terfol. He was explaining about the books and how they had begun to see things after reading them. Terfol seemed interested in this, but he had never heard of anything like it. The Gylf had nothing in their traditions about how humans gained sight. In fact, their traditions said very little at all about humans.

"There is only one mention of humans speaking with Gylf," explained Terfol. "It says that the seeing ones come who are able to see as the Gylf see and will help them in their task."

"Task?" asked Adam. "What task?"

"The task of rejoicing," said Terfol.

"Rejoicing?" Adam could not have looked more confused.

Terfol smiled. "You see all this?" He gestured at the trees and sky. "Why does it exist? It exists to bring delight, to cause joy. But this can never happen if there is no one to feel the delight, to taste the joy. This is the task of the Gylf."

After all she had seen that day, Alex thought she knew what he meant, but Adam was still looking at Terfol blankly.

"So you just…enjoy things? What do you do, just sit and look around?"

"Sometimes. But there are many ways of enjoying the world. True joy grows when it is shared. So we share it. We walk among the trees and in our walking our joy overflows in song which brings joy to the trees who listen. We gather fallen wood to make fires for the food we enjoy, and this helps to keep the forest from becoming cluttered. We aid hurting animals that we might rejoice to see them in motion again, and this becomes their salvation."

"So you look after the forest. You're like caretakers," said Adam.

"In a way," replied Terfol, "but this is not our main task. Our main task is to enjoy." Seeing that Adam still did not comprehend, he continued with a smile, "Do not worry. Many mornings begin in fog, but the sun comes and burns the mist away. You will see more clearly in time. You would not be here if it were not so."

"Come," said Celana. "The meal is ready."

She pointed to the rock, which had a fire lit in the middle, over which a large pot of soup was cooking. At least, it must have been enormous for the Gylf; for Alex and Adam it looked more like a sugar bowl. In small mounds around the fire were berries and nuts and some lumpy roots that Alex didn't recognize. There were also tiny loaves of bread being handed out by several young women.

The Gylf ate with the same enthusiasm that they danced. Each one had his own loaf of bread, but the bowls of soup were passed around and shared. Adam and Alex were included in this sharing, though of course for them it was more like sipping from a small wooden thimble. Even with such tiny portions, Alex could tell that the food was delicious. She was still hungry after everything was finished, but she decided against finding one of the sandwiches they had brought along. It just seemed too ordinary after everything else that had happened.

Celana had thought of this, however. She came to Alex and Adam after the meal leaning on the arm of a young Gylf with close-cropped grey hair and slate grey eyes. "You will not have been satisfied with our food, large as you are," she stated simply. "I do not know what you are accustomed to eating or if we are able to provide it, but we must do what we can so that you do not go hungry."

"We did actually bring some of our own food," said Adam.

"Good!" smiled Celana. "Then you must eat it. Everything has its place in this world, and our food is a delight to us, but it cannot suit you as your own food would."

"I don't think..." Alex began, but Adam was already opening his backpack and taking out a sandwich. Alex felt a brief flash of annoyance. How could he eat a plain sandwich here? Then her own stomach rumbled loudly. When Adam offered her a ham and cheese on rye, she gave in. To her surprise, she found that Celana was right; the sandwich was just the thing. She ate it hungrily and felt much better when she was done.

Celana waited politely for them to finish and then said, "Come. To mark the occasion of your first visit to us, we will show you the treasure of our forest. But we must move quickly if we are to arrive by the changing hour."

Then, with no sign of embarrassment, she turned to the young Gylf next to her, and he lifted her into his arms as if she were a baby. The whole group was moving now, filtering through the trees on the other side of the clearing.

As she and Adam followed the crowd, Alex felt again the disadvantage of her size. While the Gylf slipped between roots and branches without ever disturbing a leaf, she was lucky if she didn't trample anyone. At one point, too busy watching the gracefulness of the Gylf to notice her own feet, she tripped and would have come crashing down on the whole lot of them if Adam hadn't caught her arm.

"Do not worry," spoke up the young grey-haired Gylf. "We do not have far to go."

Alex couldn't help but think it was the Gylf who should be worried with such a clumsy giant along with them.

"I am Pidras," continued the Gylf, not showing any sign of the exertion of carrying Celana. "It is a joy to have you with us. I have long been curious about humans."

"Thank you," said Alex. "This has all been incredible. You've been so wonderful to us."

"How else should we be?" asked Pidras.

Alex had no answer to that. Instead, she asked, "Where are we going?"

"To the changing tree," said Pidras.

"What is that?"

"You must see it for yourself. No words of mine could be adequate."

Just as Pidras said, it was only another 10 minutes or so when they all emerged from the trees into a very large clearing with one enormous and beautiful tree standing in the middle. The sun was very low and a soft warm light surrounded the group of Gylf who gathered expectantly around the tree. They were all very quiet, but Alex could hear a whispering from the branches above her. She glanced up. The trees around the edge of the clearing were leaning into each other and whispering softly.

"You hear the trees speaking," said Pidras matter-of-factly.

"What? Yes... I mean, are they really talking?" asked Alex.

"Of course," Pidras replied.

"Can you understand what they are saying?"

"No. To my knowledge no one can understand the speech of the trees."

"Then how do we know it is speech and not just noises?" Adam asked.

Pidras looked puzzled. "Because they are speaking," he said. "You have seen them. You have heard them. If they choose to only speak to brother trees and not to us, that does not make their speech any less."

At a quick gesture from Celana, he fell silent and turned toward the magnificent lone tree. There was a moment when everyone in the clearing seemed to hold their breath. Then the branches began to glow. The sun had lowered to the level of the surrounding forest and its rays were lighting up the Changing Tree with increasing intensity. What began as a glow brightened until the leaves burned. They glittered and sparkled almost as if...

"The leaves are jewels!" exclaimed Alex.

There was a collective sigh of contentment from the surrounding Gylf.

"Yes," whispered Pidras. "For just this moment they are stones."

They all stood and watched the shining jewel tree until the sun sank below the tree tops and the light of the tree slowly faded.

Alex turned to say something to Adam but fell silent when she saw his face. It was alight with a glow almost as bright as the Changing Tree itself.

49

Chapter 5

A Journey of Brothers Begun

Opening the front door at home that night, Adam felt like he was waking up from a dream. There was his dad, sitting on the couch reading the paper just like he did every night. The television was on in the family room where Adam's older brother, Brian, was inevitably watching baseball. And if he wasn't mistaken, there was a bit of smoke in the air. His mom must have burnt dinner even more than usual tonight.

It was all so depressingly normal that Adam almost turned around and walked right back out the door. But he wasn't quick enough.

"Where have you been?" Sheila Cleary was high strung even on the best of days, and it was clear as she came charging out of the kitchen that this had not been the best of days. "You said you were going to friend's house, but you didn't say who, and that was six hours ago. I called your cell phone four times, and it sent me straight to voice mail. I expect better of you, Adam. I expect you to call if you are going to be gone longer than you thought. I don't have time to run all over town looking for you. I have a meeting tonight and now the dinner is ruined and the last thing I need is to be worrying about where you've run off to."

"Sorry, Mom," said Adam calmly. The only way to survive with her was to avoid giving her any fuel for the fire. It wouldn't do at all, for example, to tell her that he intentionally left his cell phone at home so that she couldn't call him. "Do you want me to call and order a pizza for dinner, so you can get ready for your meeting?"

She ran a hand distractedly through her hair. "Yes, that would probably be good."

She disappeared into the kitchen again and came back rummaging through her purse. "Here's thirty dollars. Don't forget that your dad will want onions on his. You'd better get two pizzas. Brian won't eat it with onions. And don't get any of that cinnamon stuff. It's pure fat."

"Okay, Mom." He must have let too much of his irritation creep into his voice because she turned at the bottom of the stairs.

"Don't you use that tone with me, young man. I work hard to take care of every person in this house, and you'd just better appreciate that. And you still haven't explained where you've been all afternoon. Oh, look at your shoes. Covered in dirt. Get those off and clean them up before you track it all over the house. *Where* have you been?"

"I just went walking in the woods with one of my friends," said Adam, silently cursing himself for drawing her attention.

"In what woods? With what friend?" Sheila was eyeing him suspiciously. Then she looked down at her watch and gasped. "Is it 7:30 already? Oh, I'm so late." She turned and sped up the stairs.

Saved by the clock again, thought Adam as he dumped his dirty shoes by the door. Her constant rushing around was irritating, but it did come in handy sometimes. Not that he'd been doing anything wrong, but once she found out that the friend he was with was a girl, it would lead to more questions. Not to mention trying to explain what they were doing in the woods all afternoon.

It never even occurred to Adam to tell anyone in his family about the book or the things he had seen since reading it. He couldn't remember the last time he confided anything in his dad, who worked at a bank and was...practical. His mom was okay, but she was such a basket case half the time that he would never try to get into anything this weird with her. As for Brian, he would just use this as an excuse to make fun of Adam even more. Adam was pretty sure the members of his family were the most unimaginative people on the planet. Being home for five minutes was almost enough to make *him* doubt what he had seen the last couple of days.

Two hours and five slices of pizza later, Adam threw himself into bed feeling thoroughly deflated. He couldn't wait to meet up with Alex at the circle the next day. He remembered that glow on her face after she had seen the Changing Tree, and he knew that she had felt what he did. Considering that just one day earlier he had never even met her, he already felt like she knew him better than the people he'd lived with his whole life.

* * * * *

Alex was stretched out in the shade of the largest tree in the circle when Adam arrived the next day. He could see that she had her book out, and it looked like she'd been crying. When she noticed him, she sat up, dropping the book and wiping her eyes with the back of her hand.

"Are you okay?" he asked, wondering if someone had been giving her a hard time and suddenly realizing that he didn't know anything about her family or friends or her life before last week.

"Yeah, I'm fine," she said, shaking her head to shake off the tears. "It's just the story. Sometimes it's just so perfect that it makes me cry, you know?"

Adam didn't know, but he didn't want to say so. Instead he got his own book out of his backpack and sat down next to her.

They spent a few minutes comparing the books. Except for some of the water stains, they seemed to be identical. That led to a discussion of the story they had each read and whether they had understood the same details. They had. Adam was just wondering aloud for the fifth time why they couldn't understand any more of the book when they saw someone coming across the field.

As the figure got closer, they saw that it was a skinny boy about their age, with straight dark hair that hung over his eyes slightly. He was dressed in old jeans and a t-shirt that looked a bit too big for him. So far, he hadn't seemed to notice them, though he was looking at the trees with interest.

Adam held his breath. Sure enough, as he approached the circle, the boy shrugged off an extremely shabby looking backpack and pulled out a familiar faded red book. It was all Adam could do to keep from shouting in excitement. He jumped up.

Clearly the new kid had not seen them sitting there because he started so violently that he dropped his book.

"Sorry," said Adam quickly. "Didn't mean to scare you. We were just sitting here waiting to see if anyone else would show up."

The boy looked confused.

"The book," explained Alex. "We read the same book you did. That's how we found this place. I'm Alex, and this is Adam. I think I've seen you at school before. You're Logan, right?"

"Yeah, hi," said the boy with embarrassment. "I've seen you around." He bent down to retrieve his book and stood picking at its binding for a minute. "So, uh, you guys really both read this same book?"

"Yep," said Adam, grinning and holding out his own book. "It's pretty amazing, isn't it?"

"Yeah," Logan said almost reverently.

Now Alex and Adam couldn't wait to hear his whole story and they peppered him with questions. It turned out that he had received the book the same way they had and had no more idea who had sent it than they did. He had tried to read it unsuccessfully the first night and then put it aside for a couple of days. Then two nights ago, he couldn't sleep and so picked it back up again. This time he could understand the first story. He wasn't sure what had made the difference. He hadn't been intentionally looking for the circle of trees. He was just wandering around town when he saw this place and it reminded him of the story. He, too, had been having headaches ever since reading the book. In fact, he had one right now, but it wasn't as bad as the first day.

Adam and Alex assured him that the headaches would go away. Then they asked if he'd seen any unusual things.

Logan's eyes widened. "Is that because of the book?" he asked.

"We think so," answered Alex. "At least, we've both seen some pretty crazy stuff."

"Like what?" asked Logan quietly, his eyes on the rock he was pushing with his toe.

"Whispering trees," said Adam. "Moving rocks, cloud pictures. Oh, and a whole race of tiny people living in the forest."

At this last one, Logan looked up. He didn't look shocked at all, more like relieved.

"Have you seen them, too?" Alex asked.

"No," said Logan, "but I've seen something…" He trailed off, nervously pushing his hair out of his eyes. "In the empty lot behind the...behind where I live, there's a big old tree stump. Well, more than a stump. It's like the whole trunk of a tree but with no branches or anything. It's all burned looking. The kids always use it as a backstop when they're playing baseball. But yesterday, I was out there and I noticed that on one side it has what looks like a face. I thought that was weird, but then the mouth part opened and it sighed really big. Then one of the eyes peeked open just a little bit. For a second I thought I was losing it. My head was hurting really bad that day. But when it saw that I was looking right at it, it talked."

He stopped, waiting for them to laugh.

"What did it say?" asked Adam.

Logan shrugged nervously. "Not much really. I think it was more surprised than I was. It just kept repeating that this shouldn't be happening. I asked it what it was called, and it said, 'Dund,' but I don't know if that's its name or what. Then it went back to saying that this wasn't right, and finally it told me it needed more time to think and to leave it alone. I left, and when I went back this morning, I could still see the face, but the eyes were shut and didn't open even when I shouted at it. I was starting to think I imagined the whole thing."

"I doubt it," Adam said and told him all about their visit with the Gylf the day before. When he finished, Logan looked awe-struck.

"You mean, all these things have just been living here all along but we could never see them before?"

"It looks that way," answered Adam. "And somehow reading this book made us able to see them now."

He was about to tell Logan about the tree circle being a meeting place when Alex interrupted. "Um, guys. There's someone else coming."

This time it was a girl, and Adam recognized her. Her name was Eve Sloane, and she was a grade ahead of him in school.

Adam knew you should never judge people without giving them a chance. But, like everyone, he sometimes ignored the things he knew. He felt that in this instance he could be pretty safe saying that there was no way he was ever going to like Eve Sloane. She was on the volleyball team and was very popular. He had seen her at football games, so he knew she was a cheerleader at the high school now. He'd never talked to her before, but based on the people she hung out with, he was sure she'd be vapid and boring and more than a little snobby.

Why would someone send *her* this book? And why would she read it? Maybe she didn't. Maybe it was just a coincidence that she was coming by right now.

He glanced over at Logan and saw that he was watching him with a strange look in his eyes.

"She might not be that bad, you know," Logan said softly.

Adam felt a little ashamed. He didn't know he was being so obvious. "Of course not," he said quickly.

Now Eve had seen them and came into the circle shaking her head. "This can't be what I think it is," she said without introduction. Then noticing at their books, she gasped, "It is! You all have this same crazy book. Is that why you're here?"

Adam felt his heart sink, but Alex stepped forward, holding her book up as an answer.

Eve nodded. "Me, too. Mine's at home. I found this place last night, and there was that carving on the tree, but no on was here. Still, I figured someone must have carved it, so I came back today."

"We didn't do the carving," Alex said. "We found it ourselves a couple of days ago. I'm Alex."

"Eve."

"And this is Adam and Logan," Alex pointed in turn.

"Nice to meet you," said Eve. "You look familiar," she gestured at Adam. "I must have seen you at school?"

Irritated, Adam just nodded.

The next few minutes were spent comparing stories, with Alex and Eve doing most of the talking. Eve's story was much the same as everyone else's.

"I probably wouldn't even have read the book," she said. "I don't read much that I don't have to for school." (Adam looked down so no one would see him rolling his eyes.) "But somehow the day after it was delivered, my mom got a hold of it and started freaking out asking me where I got it. I think she thought it was a book of magic spells or something, you know, because it's so old looking and the words don't make any sense. So she starts yelling about how she won't have me messing around with this sort of thing and how I don't know how dangerous it is. And then she threw it in the trash. But it made me mad because she got all upset without even bothering to find out what the book really was. And then I realized that I didn't know what it was either, so I went and got it out of the trash. It was still right on top, so I didn't have to do any digging or anything," She laughed. "And then I started to read it, but it didn't make any sense. I wondered if maybe my mom was right about it being some kind of spell or something, so I started

61

to read it out loud in my room, and when I heard it out loud, I could understand it somehow. Then I knew it was a story and nothing like what my mom was saying. But it was so awesome I just kept reading and reading until the story ended and then I couldn't understand any more of the book."

Eve had also experienced the same headaches as the others and had seen some things moving around that shouldn't have been moving. But she had just passed that off as her imagination, and she hadn't seen anything more unusual than that. *It figures*, thought Adam.

"Now that you mention it, though," she said thoughtfully, "things do seem brighter and more colorful lately. I keep stopping to look around me at stuff I've seen a hundred times before because it all of a sudden seems so beautiful. Is that the sort of stuff you guys have noticed, too?"

Alex told her that they had felt that way, too, then went on to tell about the Gylf, and Logan explained about the Dund creature he had found. When they were finished, Eve was staring at them.

Here it comes, thought Adam.

"Wow," said Eve, "That is crazy. I know I should be thinking you guys have lost it or something, but I actually believe you. You totally have to show me where these things are."

Logan and Alex agreed, but Adam felt it was time to bring a little reality back to the situation.

"If we're going to be going all over town to talk to strange creatures, we're going to need a way to explain it to our families. And don't you have friends who will be wondering what you're doing with us?"

Eve shrugged. "Yeah, they'll wonder. But most of them are super busy anyway. And I don't think I'll be getting any phone calls for a few days. I kind of showed the book to a few of my friends right after I read it, and I'm pretty sure they thought I was crazy. They couldn't understand it at all."

Adam snorted.

"Maybe you can only understand the book if it was addressed to you," suggested Alex.

"That makes sense," said Logan, then, embarrassed, he added, "at least, as much sense as any of this makes."

Eve and Alex laughed.

"Maybe," said Adam doubtfully. He couldn't help but think that Eve's friends weren't much of a test. He planned to show the book to his friend James when he came home from vacation in a couple of weeks. James and Adam almost always liked the same things, and Adam was pretty sure that James was going to flip over this book. But he didn't bother saying any of that.

"So what about our parents?" he asked.

"My dad won't even notice I'm gone," said Alex.

"And my mom won't care as long as I'm home by five to watch the kids when she goes to work," Logan added.

"So it's pretty much just our parents we have to worry about," said Eve to Adam. "The easiest thing to do with my mom is probably just to go over, you guys look all angelic, I tell her you're some new friends I've made and that we'll be hanging out, and then she'll be off my back."

"In other words, the truth," said Alex, smiling.

Eve looked like this hadn't occurred to her. "Yeah, basically, I guess you're right."

"Should we do the same thing with your parents, Adam?" asked Alex.

Adam was annoyed at the way Eve was taking charge, but since there was no good reason to feel that way, he just said, "Probably."

"Okay, then," Eve smiled. "We'll make a couple of stops at our houses and then head off to see these...what did you call them?"

"Gylf," responded Alex.

"I think we should go see the Dund thing first," said Adam.

They all looked at him.

"I mean, we don't know anything about it, so it makes sense to investigate that first."

"Maybe," began Alex slowly, "but we did promise the Gylf that we'd come back to see them."

"Yeah, but we didn't say we'd come today. If we're going to figure out what this is that's happening to us, we need to check out all the new things we find." Adam could hear how bossy he sounded and he hated it, but he couldn't seem to stop either. "The Gylf were really cool, but they didn't seem to know much about our situation. Maybe this Dund thing will know more."

"There'll be plenty of time to check everything out," said Eve. "I think if these Gylf are expecting you guys then we should go there. Anyway, didn't Logan say that Dund didn't want to talk to him?"

"Yeah, he seemed really irritated by me," confirmed Logan.

"So we'll go see the Gylf now and check out the Dund tomorrow," decided Eve.

Adam wanted to snap at her, but he could see that Alex and Logan agreed with Eve, so he swallowed it again.

They all grabbed their backpacks and followed Eve toward her house, Adam seething inside. Why did this girl have to get the book, too? She was going to be a serious pain in the butt.

Then he looked over and saw Logan smiling at him.

"She *is* a little bossy," Logan shrugged, "but seriously, did you ever think a week ago that you'd be here today arguing over which unheard of creature you wanted to visit?"

In spite of himself, Adam smiled. He could feel his irritation fade as his sense of adventure crept in to take its place.

Logan was right. With or without Eve Sloane, this was going to be the best summer of his life.

Chapter 6

Leaves in the Wind

Logan felt his heart pounding as he followed the others down the slope from the road to the forest where Alex said the Gylf lived. So far this had been the best day of his life, apart from the one sickening moment when it occurred to him that maybe these kids were playing a trick on him and any minute were all going to stop and point, laughing at him.

This was not a prank, though. Even apart from the things he'd seen himself, he could tell by looking at Alex and Adam that they weren't lying. He could see their own confusion and excitement in their eyes.

Of course, that meant that in a few short minutes he would be meeting a whole race of foot-high people who lived in the forest and, according to Alex, spent their time enjoying things. No doubt about it, this was too far out there for anyone to make up.

Adam was leading them through the trees when he suddenly stopped short. At first Logan couldn't see why, but then Alex kneeled down, and he saw the young woman on the path in front of them.

As described, she was only about ten inches tall and dressed all in green and brown with dark red berries woven into her thick brown hair, but Alex's description hadn't done her justice. She was like one of his favorite childhood fairytales brought to life. The little woman's delicate beauty took his breath away, and though he could hear Alex introducing him and Eve, he couldn't say anything. Instead, he nodded hello, fighting off the urge to bow or do something equally stupid.

The tiny beauty (he thought Alex had introduced her as Terra) was watching him with a smile. "This one speaks with his eyes instead of his tongue," she said.

He felt self-conscious as the others glanced at him, but Terra began talking of other things, and he was soon drawn back in to the conversation.

"There won't be many at our home today. Word came early this morning that the vines have reached full strength, so all who were not otherwise occupied are heading to the gully to swing. I am going there myself, though I was delayed by the discovery of these berries which the birds had left behind. If you wish to come with me, I know that you would all be welcome at the vine swinging."

No one had any objection. Terra shimmied up a tree and began to skip along the branches, hopping lightly from tree to tree leading them off the path and further into the forest. They hurried after her, Logan once again bringing up the rear.

As he crunched along, he found himself imagining the life of these little Gylf and how wonderful it must be, living all together with no worries and all this beauty around them every day. He was just picturing Terra waking up in the morning inside a beautiful bedroom carved out of a tree trunk and lined with soft moss when he realized that the others were getting too far ahead. Better save the daydreams for some other time or he'd be seriously lost. It wouldn't be the first time that his daydreaming had got him into trouble, but he didn't want to miss anything today.

Terra finally came to a stop at the edge of a large crease in the earth. On all sides massive trees stood like old men trailing long cloaks of vines. No trees grew in the gully itself, but the slope was covered in foliage and there were large heaps of dead leaves along the bottom. He heard the cries of greeting before his eyes had registered the large number of Gylf in the trees on every side.

It was a bit startling to realize that they were surrounded by people, but for Logan, it was like suddenly having one of his daydreams become a reality. Of course, that would be unpleasant for some people, but Logan's daydreams were all better than his real life, so for him it was a wonderful feeling.

After a flurry of greetings and introductions, in which Logan caught almost no names, the Gylf showed the kids how the vine swinging was done. Choosing a vine that hung free over the gully, one Gylf would tie the end around his waist and then climb to a secure branch, pulling the vine taut. Up to ten other Gylf would then scamper up the tree and onto the same vine. When all were in place and clinging tightly to the vine, the anchor would let go of the tree, and the whole group would swing out laughing over the ravine.

The Gylf seemed completely fearless. Many would grip the vine with their legs and clap and wave their arms as they swung, and a few even waited until the vine had swung out to its farthest point and then leapt from the vine onto a tree on the opposite side of the ravine. This feat was met with cheers from those on the ground.

It all looked like so much fun that inevitably the kids began to discuss trying out the vines themselves. The Gylf couldn't offer any advice since they knew very little about humans and had never considered anyone swinging on vines but themselves. Alex had some doubts that it would be safe for them with their greater weight (and Logan was secretly inclined to agree with her), but Eve dismissed this objection. She had been vine swinging in the woods with some friends before, and no one had fallen, she said.

"Besides," she added. "What's the worst that could happen? We fall onto those big piles of leaves. It looks like it wouldn't even hurt."

"That's not really the worst that could happen," replied Adam with an eye roll that made Logan cringe, "but yeah, the vines look really strong. You guys don't have to do it, but I want to go at least once."

In the end, it was agreed that they'd let the Gylf pick the very strongest vine and then Adam and Eve would take turns testing it. If it worked for them, Alex consented to try it, too. Logan said very little during all of this conversation. He wanted very badly to swing on the vine, but the prospect of falling and breaking a bone was an ugly one. He didn't want to seem like a coward, but visions of blood and limbs twisted at unnatural angles came unbidden to his mind. Sometimes he wished he could just turn his imagination off, but those were always the times when it was least possible.

Having decided, they lost no time in getting started. A fine, strong vine was chosen, and away went Adam, whooping and laughing over the ravine. Eve was next and slid off the vine breathless and shining-eyed after her ride. The vine seemed to be holding up well, and since Logan was even lighter than the first two he felt confident to take his own turn.

He gripped the vine firmly as Terra showed him, stepped back for a running start, and then swung out into open air. It was exhilarating, like flying. Hearing the laughter of the Gylf swinging on other vines nearby, he felt a bubble of happiness swell inside him. He flashed a quick grin at Alex as he swung back past the others on the high ground and out again over the gully.

Of course, it was too good to last. On his third swing out, just as he reached the farthest point, Logan heard a sickening pop over his head. For a split second, he didn't register what was happening and then he was falling, vine still clutched in his hand. He heard someone scream, he wasn't sure who, and then he hit the ground hard on his side.

A moment passed while he just lay there without moving, a pain throbbing in his side, and then he sat up. Just as Eve had predicted, the piles of leaves had mostly broken his fall, but something very hard had struck him just above his hip. Craning his head around, he could see an angry red mark that would soon be a nasty bruise.

"I'm okay," he called out to the others, pushing the leaves aside to see what he had landed on. Something shiny caught his eye, and he pulled out what looked like an old trophy, a two-handled metal cup all rusted over. What a weird thing to be in the middle of the woods.

By that time, the others had managed to scramble down into the gully and were coming towards him. He could see the look of alarm on Alex's face and of guilt on Eve's. The Gylf also wore concerned looks as they dropped lightly from the vines onto the leaves around him. Adam brought up the rear, and Logan could tell by his expression that he was just waiting to be told that there was no injury so he could laugh over how funny the fall had been.

"I'm really fine," Logan reassured them. "No big deal. I just hit this and bruised myself a little." He held up the cup.

Once they had seen for themselves that Logan was not hurt, everyone was very interested in the trophy he had found. A little investigation led to the discovery of a few other objects nearby: a corroded tin bowl, a thin rusty chain, several broken pens and pencils, and countless scraps of paper, soggy and unrecognizable.

Then Adam gave an excited cry. He had wandered further along the gully away from the main cluster of vines to where a large rock blocked off one end. There around the base of the rock was a whole pile of old rusty junk. Logan thought that people had just been throwing trash down here, but Adam was pointing to one of the items half buried under the refuse. It was a sword, quite rusty but seemingly still in one piece.

They all stood looking at it for a minute. Something prickled on the back of Logan's neck. His eyes told him that he was looking at an ordinary pile of junk in the woods, but he couldn't shake the feeling that something was off.

Eve was asking the Gylf about this place.

"We do not know what all these things are," answered a young man whose name Logan could not remember. "We never come to this rock."

"Why not?" asked Logan.

"For no reason that I know," the young man said. "We simply do not come here."

"Is it off limits or something?" wondered Eve.

"No, it is not forbidden," he replied. "There is nothing for us here."

Suddenly Alex called out commandingly, "Stop!"

Adam had begun to climb up the pile of junk. He paused as everyone stared in surprise at Alex. She wore a very strange expression. It seemed to Logan that she was looking at something that no one else could see.

"I'm just going to get that sword," said Adam.

"Don't," insisted Alex. "It's not safe."

Adam cocked his head as he surveyed the pile. "It's fine." He stamped his foot. "It's a pretty sturdy pile actually."

"I mean it," Alex held firm. "Don't climb it."

But Adam had turned his back on her. He was almost to the sword now. Logan found himself holding his breath. Adam was standing over the sword now. He bent down and tugged, but it was wedged between two pieces of junk so rusty it was impossible to tell what they were. Adam leaned one arm against the giant rock to get some leverage and pulled hard. There was a crunching noise, and then the earth next to the rock caved in pulling half the pile crashing and clanking with it. Adam yelped as he was knocked off his feet.

It was all over in a matter of moments, and when the dust settled everyone was relieved to see Adam's head still sticking out of the ground. He was clinging to the edge of the hole that had opened around him.

Immediately several Gylf rushed toward him.

"Do you think it's safe?" asked Eve, looking at Alex.

"Safe or not," replied Alex, "we can't just leave him there. The Gylf will never be able to get him out by themselves."

They all stepped gingerly onto what was left of the junk pile and picked their way over to Adam. When they got there, they saw that things were not as bad as they had looked. Adam was not hanging in the hole but rather standing on the pile of garbage which had fallen below him. It was just far enough down that he couldn't climb out, but at least he wasn't in any danger of falling further in. Logan and Eve each grabbed a hand and pulled, allowing him to scramble his way out. When Adam finally collapsed breathless beside them, they all looked at each other silently for a moment. Adam's legs were cut and scraped, but other than that he seemed unharmed.

"I guess I owe you a serious apology," he said finally to Alex. "I should have listened to you."

Alex didn't answer, but Logan thought she looked more thoughtful than angry.

"How did you know that was going to happen?" Eve asked her.

Alex shrugged. "I don't know. It just didn't seem safe to me."

"But you were so sure," Eve insisted.

Alex nodded but didn't say anything.

"Well, however you knew," said Adam, "I'm never ignoring your advice again." He gave her a smile that seemed to Logan to be asking for some sign of forgiveness.

Alex half-smiled back but was still very preoccupied with her own thoughts.

Now the Gylf, who had stepped out of the way while Adam was being pulled out of the hole and for the last several minutes had been holding a huddled conference in low voices, approached them.

Terra spoke for the group. "We have been discussing our situation and what is appropriate to do next. It seems to us that the reason no Gylf come here may be greater than we realized. We do not know what this place is, but it is clearly not a natural part of the forest. We will ask the grandfathers, but we who are here are agreed that it would be better to leave this place alone in the future. For now, our most important concern is healing your injuries. Unfortunately, we do not have any skill at nursing humans. Perhaps you can tell us what is best to be done."

"I'm okay," said Adam. "Don't worry about me."

"You should get those cuts cleaned," said Eve. "There was a lot of rust on that stuff. You could get infected."

Adam was about to object, but Alex said, "She's right. You're a mess. I have antibiotic stuff at my house if you want to clean up so your mom doesn't see you like that. She didn't seem like the type who would want you bleeding on her carpet."

Having just said he'd always listen to Alex's advice, Adam could hardly argue.

Logan felt disappointed that they weren't going to see the Gylf's home. He knew that they could come back another day, but he hated to head back to the ordinary world after so short a time here. The thought of going home to the dirty trailer park where he lived was repugnant.

Still, he could tell by Adam's expression as he stood up that he was in more pain than he let on, so Logan tried not to be selfish and shouldered his backpack along with the others.

Terra accompanied the children to the edge of the woods. As she gracefully stepped along a branch near him, Logan was amazed at the incredible way that she fit into the loveliness of the forest. Each branch and leaf and fern was pulsating with life, and this little woman was the walking expression of that life.

Finally, after the fifth time she caught him staring, Terra laughed lightly and said, "I can see why sight was given to you. Your eyes speak of their joy in the beauty around them."

Logan hesitated but then asked, "What exactly is this... sight?"

She stopped and tilted her head a bit. "You see, don't you?"

"Yes."

"And most humans do not."

He thought he knew what she meant, but he felt the need to have it put into words for him. "But it's not like people are blind. They can see. They read. They write. They walk around without bumping into things."

"True," she laid one slender hand on the tree trunk next to her. "But when they see this, what do they see?"

"A tree."

"Yes. And when you see it, what do you see?"

Logan looked at the tree. He wanted desperately to say something profound, but he didn't know how. "A tree, but..."

But what? he thought. There weren't words for what he felt as he touched the tough, knobbly skin, as he felt the life pulsing through that strong trunk, as he looked up at the graceful branches stretching out to embrace the sky in an ecstasy of green.

Terra smiled. "Exactly. A tree, but... That is sight."

The others had stopped and were waiting, so Logan turned and continued walking silently.

As the kids said goodbye to Terra and promised to come back soon to visit, Logan found his reluctance to leave settling into depression. Then he felt Terra press something into his hand. He looked down. It was the wreath of berries that she had been wearing in her hair.

"A gift for the quiet one with the talking eyes," she said.

"Oh, uh, thank you," he stuttered. "You didn't have to..."

"It increases my joy to see your pleasure in them," she smiled. "Now they bring joy to more than myself."

Strangely, as he followed the others back to the road, Logan did feel a sense of joy. This wasn't just one of his daydreams. This was real, and it would keep being real. Even if most of the world was boring and ugly, there were still truly beautiful places. Now he had seen one with his own eyes, and he had only to look down at the berries in his hand to remember it.

Chapter 7

Muttering Over and Over

The following day found the kids tripping across the abandoned lot behind the trailer park where Logan lived. Eve looked around and laughed to herself. If her friends could see where she was and who she was with, they would have a few things to say about it. For some reason, that didn't bother her. In fact, it sort of added to her sense of excitement about this new adventure. You could bet that none of them were doing anything half so interesting right now. She tried to imagine her essay on "What I did this summer" and chuckled out loud.

These last couple of days had been like nothing she could have imagined. She had never read the kinds of books that would have made her picture herself meeting miniature people living in the woods or discovering secret hieroglyphics in the clouds or sharing mysterious headaches with a group of weird kids she'd never met before.

Not that these kids were at all bad or anything. They'd actually been really nice. They were smart and fun, a combination she didn't previously know existed. Eve was relieved to be with other people who understood what was happening to her, even though she still couldn't shake the desire to laugh sometimes at how seriously they were taking everything.

This morning had been one of those times.

They had all met at the circle of trees again, and Adam had started in right away. He wanted to name the circle of trees. If it was going to be their main meeting spot, it should have a name, he said. Everyone agreed that it was a good idea, but coming up with a name was harder than it sounded.

Alex suggested the Circle of Seeing or the Ring of Renown. But those both seemed a bit long and heavy. Eve thought maybe something simple like The Aspens would be better, but Adam said that sounded like the name of a golf club.

"The Gylf would probably just call it Home," said Logan.

"Yeah, but we don't actually live here," Eve pointed out, "so that might get a little confusing."

They all fell silent.

"The Redoubt," said Adam under his breath.

"What?" asked Eve.

Adam shrugged. "The Redoubt. I read this book once where this army was defending its home city against an enemy with way more soldiers, and they had a place, like a tower but hidden in the forest, where they could go to rest and they wouldn't be found, and it was called a redoubt. I only remember it because it was a word I'd never heard before."

"The Redoubt," said Alex. "I like it."

So it was decided, and Eve had to admit she liked the feel of the word. It stood out in her mind in all capitals: REDOUBT, sounding strong and safe.

There is something about naming a place that makes it seem so much more friendly, and the kids had felt quite at home in the breezy circle of trees as they whiled away the morning comparing their books and watching the cloud pictures and waiting to see if anyone else would turn up. No one had, though, and they decided after lunch to go and check out Logan's Dund.

Eve could see Logan now, pointing to something on the opposite end of the field. It looked like a burned out tree trunk, still standing, but with no branches or leaves. On closer view, this impression held true. She could even see the gnarled roots and a few scorch marks on the bark. It was so ordinary looking that if she hadn't just met a bunch of miniature people the day before, she would have thought that Logan had imagined the whole thing. Even as it was, she wasn't sure.

They all gathered around as Logan said tentatively, "Excuse me."

There was no movement or sound.

"Excuse me," he said a little louder.

When there was still no response, he looked a little ashamedly at the others.

"How did it talk to you before?" asked Alex.

Logan pointed out what could possibly be taken for a mouth and eyes. Of course, it could also be taken for random patterns in the bark, thought Eve.

Alex stepped up close and said firmly, "We know you can hear us. And we know you can talk. So stop pretending. We'd like to talk to you."

Again Eve pictured what people would think if they could see her right now. But then she gave a little jump. She had seen an eye crack open. It closed again, but she was sure of what she'd seen.

"We saw that," said Adam.

This time both eyes opened, darker brown than the rest of the bark and completely unreadable.

"Bless me, there are more of them this time!" the creature said.

Its voice was high pitched and nasal and so out of keeping with its appearance that Eve struggled to suppress a laugh.

"We'd like to ask you a few questions," Adam said.

"Ask me a few questions?" it repeated. "'Ask and you shall receive,' is my motto, so ask away. Answers can be tough, though. Some things are 'easier said than done.' Still, 'where there's a will, there's a way' is my motto, so we'll give it a try."

Eve traded a bemused look with Alex. Even Adam was momentarily at a loss.

"Um, did you say your name was Dund?" asked Logan, who obviously felt responsible for this weird conversation.

"My name? No. Not my name. Dund is what I am. 'I think therefore I am.' And what I am is Dund. I don't have what you would call a

85

name." For just a moment he looked sad about this. "But then, 'What's in a name? A rose by any other name would smell as sweet.'" This seemed to cheer him up again. "I have no name, but I do have very nice skin. Perhaps you noticed? 'Make the most of what you've got' is my motto, and I make the most of my skin. No other Dund has skin quite as nice. Not that I let that go to my head. Oh, no. 'Handsome is as handsome does' is my motto, and I always try to live up to my skin. 'Beauty is only skin deep,' but I think that…"

"So there are other Dunds?" interrupted Adam eagerly.

"If there are, I've never seen them," the Dund responded, unfazed by the interruption. "'Seeing is believing,' so I suppose I don't believe in other Dunds. But 'Birds of a feather flock together,' so if I am here I suppose other Dunds are, too."

"But you said no other Dund has skin as nice as yours," protested Adam, while Eve wondered if the Dund had any idea what it was talking about.

"And so they haven't. Have you ever seen a Dund with skin so nice and brown and wrinkly?" the Dund asked.

Adam seemed unable to answer this question, and the Dund began to look offended. Alex giggled.

"Your skin is lovely," said Eve. After all, someone had to say something. "It's my very favorite shade of brown."

The Dund fairly beamed. "So I've often thought myself. I do a lot of thinking, you know. 'Think before you speak' is my motto, though I must say it is so much nicer to have someone to talk with than I thought it would be. 'Silence is golden' and 'children should be seen and not heard.' But 'it takes two to tango' and 'two heads are better than one,' and I have been alone a very long time. It is very nice to meet you all. What are your names?"

Eve introduced them all.

"So how long have you been here?" asked Logan curiously.

"Oh dear, that's hard to say. 'Time flies,' you know. But I guess you would say I've been here forever. From 'time immemorial.' I've never not been here. I've never been anywhere else but here. Once I thought of trying someplace else. "The grass is always greener on the other side of the fence,' you know. But 'the first step is always the hardest.' Especially for me because I can't exactly move. So here I am. And I like it. 'There's no place like home' is my motto."

"So you...were born here," said Adam. "Or, um, I mean, you grew here."

"Did I?" the Dund seemed legitimately puzzled. "I really don't remember. 'The mind is the first to go,' you know. If I grew or was born the memory is gone. The first day I remember was just like today, standing and listening and listening. Except today I am talking to you. Hmm... 'Wonders never cease,' as they say. 'Live and learn' is my motto. 'Each new day brings its own surprises.'"

"So you never spoke to anyone before?" Alex asked.

"'Speak when you are spoken to' is my motto," intoned the Dund in his ridiculously high voice. "And no one ever spoke to me. Lots of talking... 'every bird loves to hear himself sing'...but never to me. I suppose no one knew I was listening. But 'walls have ears,' you know. And I am just like a wall in that respect. I never thought an occasion for talking to anyone other than myself would come, you know, but today it has. 'There is a time and a place for everything,' you know."

"Do you have any idea why we are able to notice you listening when no one else did?" asked Logan.

"None at all. I was hoping you would tell me. Still, 'patience is a virtue,' they say, and I don't like to pry. 'Mind your own business' is my motto."

"You can ask us anything you like," said Eve smiling. She found herself liking this Dund creature, in spite of its ridiculous way of talking. "After all, we're asking you lots of questions. But the truth is we were hoping you would know something about it that we don't."

"Show him the book," Alex suggested.

Eve dug her copy of the book out of her bag. "We all had this book delivered to us, and since we read it we've been able to see stuff we never saw before. We think maybe that's why we could recognize you. Have you ever heard of anything like that?"

"Well now, let's see. I'd need to know a little more. 'Don't judge a book by its cover' is my motto. 'Appearances are deceptive.' But 'the proof of the pudding is in the tasting.' Could you read me a bit of the book?"

For a second, it occurred to Eve that she was going to sound ridiculous reading all those nonsense words out loud in front of other people. It was one thing in the privacy of her own room, but outside it was downright embarrassing. No one else was volunteering to read it, either, she noticed. Finally she realized that it would be even more awkward to refuse, so she shrugged and, opening to the first page, began to read.

At the end of the opening paragraph, she paused and glanced up. A startling change had come over the Dund's face. Whereas before his expression had been somewhat blank and his eyes unreadable, now he had the look of dawning discovery and a little flicker of memory in the brown depths of his eyes. Glancing around, Eve saw that Alex had gotten out her own book and was apparently reading along, Adam was staring at the ground, but Logan was studying the Dund's face intently, watching the same transformation that Eve had noticed.

As Eve's pause lengthened, Alex looked up. "Do you recognize that?" she asked the Dund.

"Of course, of course," he almost squeaked, a little shiver going over his whole trunk. "'It's as plain as the nose on your face.' Everyone knows the language of awakening."

"So it *is* a language!" exclaimed Adam wonderingly. "And you speak it? But then how did we understand it when none of us has ever learned it?"

"Hold your horses, there, young man. Don't put words in my mouth. I never said I *speak* the language of awakening. I said I know it. Everyone knows it. You know it. Though you didn't know you knew it, as you say. But 'the proof of the pudding is in the tasting,' as I said, and you understood this book, so it is clear that you know the language."

90

"And do you know what this book is called?" asked Alex.

"You've put your finger on it there," said the Dund. "You have hit the nail on the head. It may be that I do know its name, but can't be sure. 'Don't jump to conclusions' is my motto. So don't get your hopes up. Better to keep all hopes down. Still, wait just a bit (patience is a virtue, you know) and I will tell you something I heard once."

He paused for a moment as if trying to remember each detail of his story. Eve waited, fascinated.

"It was late in the afternoon," he continued in such a different tone that they all stared, "must have been many years ago now. A young man, older than you children but still quite young with brown hair and brown skin (lovely skin, I thought at the time), was walking through this field. He would have passed right by me, I think, but just as he arrived at this spot, another man, older and fairer, came dashing towards him from the opposite direction. The young man stopped and waited. When the older man reached us, he was panting from his sprint and it was several moments before he could speak. When he had caught his breath, he said to the young man, 'They found it. Cristina said to tell you right away.' And the young man said, 'Are you sure it's the one we're looking for?'

'Yes,' replied his friend, 'it has all the signs.' The young man began to look excited. 'We should all meet tonight then.' 'So soon?' asked the other, frightened. 'There is no time to lose,' responded the young man. 'We have to get back what he took from us. We have to find the Book of Sight. Without it the language of awakening is lost to us.' 'But we still don't know what this pilpi creature may be capable of!' argued the older man. 'Gendel sea, Harold,' whispered the young man. And he repeated, 'gendel sea.' And then the two walked away together."

There was a silence as the kids each tried to digest this new information.

"Gendel sea," said Eve after a moment. They all nodded. *Gendel sea,* part of the prophecy from the story. Just saying the words out loud again made Eve's heart swell.

"Do you think they were talking about this book?" said Adam. "The Book of Sight?"

"The name does fit," Alex said.

"But who were those men? If they live around here, they could answer a lot of our questions."

Turning to the Dund, Adam demanded, "Is that all you remember? Did you ever see them again?"

"I only saw them that one time. I thought at the time it was very interesting, and I waited to see if they would come back. But 'the watched pot never boils,' you know, and they never returned. After a while I forgot about it. 'Out of sight, out of mind,' you know. But when you read from that book it came back to me."

"What do you suppose the pilpi thing was he was talking about?" asked Logan. "There wasn't anything like that in the story, was there?"

"No," said Adam, "although it might be farther along in the book. None of us has read more than the first part."

"Whatever it is, it sounded like the older man was scared of it," said Alex. "That makes it seem more like it was something they met, not just something in a story."

"And they were going to see it," Logan added. "And they never came back."

"They never came back here, but that doesn't mean anything happened to them," protested Adam. "They never met here intentionally in the first place. Why would they have come back here again? Obviously they didn't know about the Dund."

Eve was irritated at Adam's tone. "I wouldn't say that anything here is exactly obvious," she said. "We don't know anything for sure, and we won't unless we happen to meet those men some day."

She could feel Adam bristle, but his words belied any anger he might feel. "Eve's right. The main point is that this "Book of Sight" must be the red book, and we need to find anyone else who may have it. If there are others, they might know more than we do. Then we could figure out what's going on."

"But I don't know how we do that besides just waiting in the circle of trees," said Alex.

They all fell silent again.

"Well, as I said before, 'patience is a virtue,' filled in the Dund. "Waiting isn't so bad, you know. Take it from me. I can tell you all about waiting. 'Straight from the horse's mouth,' as they say."

"I know, but I feel like we're supposed to *do* something," said Alex.

"That may be, that may be. They do say that man is always the pot-stirrer, the rabble-rouser, the dangerous one. 'Man is born to trouble as sparks fly upward.' So I suppose you'll do as men do. 'The apple doesn't fall far from the tree,' you know. Still, watch and wait, watch and wait, is my motto, and there could be worse."

None of the kids answered that.

"Well," broke out Adam finally. "If that's the only option we have, we'd better get back there. We could be missing someone right now."

He made as if to walk away, but Eve turned to the Dund. "Thank you so much for talking with us. You were very helpful."

"Oh, well," blustered the Dund, "Of course, of course. 'A friend in need is a friend indeed' is my motto. I was very glad to talk with you all. It was a very interesting experience. "Don't knock it until you've tried it' is my motto, and I'm glad I've tried this at least once. I always say…"

"We need to go now," Eve interrupted, "but we'll definitely come back and talk again sometime, okay?"

"Of course, of course, fine, fine. 'Parting is such sweet sorrow,' as they say, and I can't say about the sweetness but I am sorry to see you go. Still, 'absence makes the heart grow fonder,' you know, so I'm sure we'll all soon be very fond. And if you'll come back again, as you say… well, that would be very nice."

"We will come back," said Alex. "It was very nice to meet you."

The boys repeated this, and the Dund watched them away with a smile. Still, Eve felt sorry for him standing there immovable and alone. He had obviously enjoyed talking to them.

She couldn't even imagine not ever talking to anyone, just listening and listening and being ignored. It was too awful to think about. They would have to come back and visit him again very soon. And not just for him, either. Someone that listened that much was bound to know a lot if they just knew what questions to ask.

Her thoughts strayed to the conversation he had recounted for them. It was comforting to know that there were others who had read this book and probably experienced similar things to what they were going through now. It was not so comforting to hear that there was something out there they were afraid of, though.

In all the excitement over the new things she'd been discovering, it hadn't really occurred to her that there might be dangers, too. Or enemies even. Now that she thought of it, it seemed pretty obvious (after all someone had to be keeping this stuff a secret from everyone), but it was disturbing. It gave everything a new edge.

It made her more interested in these other kids, too. Her desire to laugh at their earnestness seemed stupid now. She thought of Alex's eerie intuition about the danger on the junk pile, of Adam's insatiable curiosity and quick thinking, and of that way Logan had of looking at you like he was reading your mind. If there was some sort of danger out there, they were going to be the ones facing it with her.

Eve was happy to realize that she had no problem with that at all.

Chapter 8

Hurrying Along, Stumbling Again

The old sword shone in the bright sunlight coming through the window. Adam turned it this way and that, marveling again, as he had so many times since that day he had first read the Book of Sight, at the way the light tripped and danced and played tag with the shadows like a living thing. He was waiting in his room for the others, who were coming over to see the newly cleaned up sword.

Two weeks had passed since the day they first visited the Dund, and still no one new had come to the ring of trees, and they had made no progress in discovering anyone else who knew anything about the Book of Sight. Mostly, the kids tried to stay close to the Redoubt, waiting for anyone new. But they had also made a few more visits to the Gylf and to the Dund. Their latest visit to the Gylf had been yesterday and when they had passed the place where they had swung on the vines, Adam had told them about the sword.

With great difficulty he had smuggled it into his house when his mother wasn't looking, and he had spent a lot of hours since then scouring off the rust. It was undeniably cool to have his own sword, even if it wasn't a particularly dangerous one. Adam had searched the internet, and he was pretty sure it was a foot artillery sword from the civil war era. It was short and straight and had a brass hilt. From what he'd read, it was more of a weed-whacker than a weapon, but it was still pretty sweet to have an antique sword hidden in his room. He was looking forward to showing it off to his friends.

Though he really wanted them to see it, he didn't want to risk smuggling it out of the house and back in again. As long as it was in his room, his mom would never find it. Other than the occasional harangue about cleaning it up, she was too busy to bother much with his room, but in other places around the house she had a disturbing tendency to pop up when you least expected her. A sword wasn't exactly something you could stick in a backpack or tuck out of sight under a sweatshirt, so they'd arranged for everyone to come by his house after meeting up at the Redoubt that morning.

Right on time, the doorbell rang. Stashing the sword carefully under his bed, Adam ran down and opened the door. Then he stopped short.

Instead of Alex, Logan and Eve, it was his best friend James waiting there. Adam quickly recovered.

"Dude! You're back!"

James grinned and stepped inside. "Didn't you get my text?"

Adam shrugged, realizing that he hadn't turned his phone on in days, and James laughed and headed automatically upstairs to Adam's room. James and Adam had been best friends since they were in kindergarten. They played video games, traded books, and liked all the same movies. James was over at Adam's house so much, he practically lived there.

"Yeah, I should have known better. So, what have you been up to?"

Adam didn't even know where to start, but he was temporarily saved from the necessity when the doorbell rang again. This time it really was Alex, Eve, and Logan.

"No one was there again," said Alex. "I'm starting to think..." She broke off as she saw James over Adam's shoulder.

To cover the awkwardness, Adam quickly invited them all inside and started on the introductions. "This is my friend, James. He's been on vacation the last couple of weeks in Florida. James, this is Alex and Logan and Eve." James's eyes registered their surprise at Eve's name. "They're...well, we just met a few weeks ago." He glanced toward the family room where the television could be heard. "Let's head up to my room, and I'll tell you about it."

All the way up the stairs, Adam's mind was racing. He had been looking forward to showing the Book of Sight to James and to having him read it. But now that the moment was here, he felt nervous. For the first time, it occurred to him that James might think he was a little crazy. He tried not to think about that. After all, James had been his friend forever, and they pretty much always agreed. He was bound to be excited about all the possibilities here. It was stupid to feel weird about it. Still, it would have been nice if he could have persuaded that twisting in his stomach to go away.

Once they were all settled in Adam's room and the door was closed, Adam turned to James. "So, this is pretty nuts," he began, and he told James all about the man delivering the book and how it seemed like nonsense at first but eventually made sense. "These guys all got the same book on the same day, and since then there have been a lot of weird things happening."

He looked around at the other kids. Eve was fiddling with the zipper of her backpack, and Alex was staring at the floor. Logan was watching James, who wore a closed and guarded expression that made Adam nervous.

"Just read the book," Adam ended lamely. "It may take some time, but once you can read it, you'll see what I mean."

James opened the book and studied the first page. He glanced back to Adam a second later. "Is this some kind of joke? It doesn't make any sense."

"I know. That's what I said. It's like that at first, but then you'll see it."

James just kept staring at him like someone waiting for a punchline.

To Adam's relief, Logan spoke up. "We know how it looks. It was like that for all of us at first. But Adam's not lying, and this isn't a joke. It's a story, and you're going to really like it."

His endorsement didn't seem to help at all. If anything, James now looked more uncomfortable.

After a pause, Adam said, "Um, so you guys want to see the sword?"

There was a general motion of assent, but he still noticed that no one was really looking at anyone else. Even Logan shifted his gaze and was now staring out the window. Obviously it was going to take time for everyone to get used to each other. Determined to break through the tension in the room, he pulled the sword from its hiding place under the bed, talking all the while.

"It took me forever to get all the rust off. It was in pretty bad shape. But I finally found this solution that worked really well. I was surprised how great it looked when I was done."

The complete lack of any response was beginning to get to him. Eve was nodding along a bit, and Alex and Logan were at least examining the sword, but James was actually looking away. Adam was irritated. Still, he carried on as if he hadn't noticed. "I've checked out the style of the sword, and it seems to me like it's a civil war era short sword. It looks almost exactly like the pictures I've seen, but they were all just drawings, so I can't be sure. Plus, I don't know if it is actually that old or if it's some sort of remake, but it's still pretty cool."

Abruptly, James broke in. "Hey man, I've got to go. I just came by to tell you I was home and see what was up. My mom's expecting me to do some chores."

"Okay," said Adam slowly, trying to ignore the wrench in his stomach and painfully aware that Logan was watching him again. "Well, take the book. We can talk when you've read it." *When you've figured it out,* he was thinking. After all, it wasn't fair to expect James to get it all yet. They had all had time to read the book and let it do its work.

"Sure," James said. "See you, everybody."

"Bye," said Alex.

"Nice to meet you," added Eve.

Once James was gone, the air in the room was ten times clearer. No one mentioned him, but they all were suddenly much more excited about the sword.

"I can't believe it's the same one you found in the woods," said Alex. "You must have done so much work to get it looking like this."

"It would be awesome if was some kind of antique," Eve said. "I wonder if we can find someone who knows about stuff like that to take it to."

Logan lifted the sword and admired the way the light from the window seemed to leap off its smooth surface.

Adam felt his frustration with James fading in the light of their enthusiasm. They spent some time speculating on where it might have come

105

from and how it might have ended up in the junk pile.

"There's something about the sword that just adds to the storybook feeling, you know?" said Alex once they finally gave up trying to figure it out. "I mean, our lives have turned into some sort of fairytale: a group of friends, strange new creatures, and now a mysterious sword. Sometimes I feel like I'm just going to wake up and find out that I'm actually sitting in fourth period math and this was all an elaborate daydream."

"But wouldn't a day dream have hotter guys in it?" Eve flipped.

"Ouch," said Logan, and Adam rolled his eyes, trying not to feel real resentment.

True, Eve had turned out to not be as bad as he had thought, but she still had this way of making him feel like he was way out of his league. And who was she to think she was all that? She might be some sort of queen at school, but this wasn't school. This was real life. And while he'd been discovering swords and organizing their explorations, what had she done?

That thought reminded him of what he'd planned to do today. "I'm thinking it's time to see if there's some other way to find people who have read the book. The Gylf and the Dund obviously don't know too much, and nothing new has turned up. If we're ever going to get to the bottom of what this book is and where it came from, we need to find people who know something. We've been waiting at the redoubt for two weeks and no one else has showed. Maybe we need to go looking."

"Sure, but how do we do that?" asked Eve. "It's not like people who have read the book have some kind of mark on their foreheads."

"Obviously," said Adam. "But I was thinking about it. Maybe we need to post some signs. Something that only someone who had read the book would understand."

"You mean like advertise or something?" Alex asked.

"Yeah, something like that."

"It's not a bad idea," Eve said. "We could make it an invitation to a meeting."

"*Gendel sea*," said Logan. "Put that on a sign and anyone who knows the story will be interested."

"That's perfect," said Alex. "And then under that just the place and the time with no information, so no one who didn't recognize it would see any reason to show up. I can't believe we didn't think of this before."

It was like magic, Adam thought, feeling the energy of an idea taking life of its own. More

107

and more lately, they all seemed to be building off of each others thoughts.

"Yeah," Eve added. "We don't want to have to explain ourselves to a bunch of people unless it's absolutely necessary."

Adam stiffened, and a silence fell as everyone was obviously thinking about James. Why did Eve always have to rub the joy off of everything? Was she doing it on purpose, or was she just a colossal idiot?

"Where should we have the meeting?" Logan broke the silence.

Eve was ready with the suggestion that she would reserve a classroom in the basement of the library. They settled it that Logan would make the signs, and they'd all hang them the next day. Alex had some great ideas about where to post them.

They decided the meeting would be the following Saturday, and then they all sat back and smiled at each other. This little plan they created was not particularly exciting or brilliant, but everyone in the room felt its rightness. Other than a few visits to the Dund and the Gylf, most of the last couple of weeks had been spent hanging around at the Redoubt, not doing much.

Now, for the first time they were actively trying to make something happen, and they all felt the difference.

Chapter 9

In the Hall of a Once Beautiful Home

Walking away from Adam's house, Eve cursed herself for her stupid comment about not wanting to explain themselves. She hadn't even been thinking about his friend until it came out, but she had seen how it offended him. Why, oh why was she always opening her big mouth without pausing to think first? She didn't want to make him feel bad. Adam could be condescending, and he obviously liked to be in charge of things, but overall she really liked him. He was smart, smarter than most. His idea about posting signs was pure genius. It was definitely time to make some new progress on figuring out this craziness.

As she headed toward the library, she said a prayer that the excitement of finding others who had read the book would help Adam deal with his friend's reaction. It was pretty obvious where that one was going.

Sure enough, the next morning when Adam arrived at the Redoubt, there was no mistaking his glowering look. He responded to Eve's good morning with a grunt, and slapped his backpack down next to Alex like it was a mouthy little sister.

After rummaging through it for a couple of minutes with increasing frustration, he swore. "I can't believe I left the stupid book on the table at home."

"You're looking a little tense there, Adam," Eve commented.

"Very observant, as always," he snapped.

Eve was glad he didn't choose to be mean too often. He was quite good at it.

"Did something happen?" she asked.

"James brought your book back, didn't he?" said Logan from behind her. Eve hadn't even noticed that he'd arrived.

"Yeah," said Adam.

"It didn't go well?" asked Alex.

Adam shrugged, but it was an angry motion. "Yeah, he was just...I don't know. Whatever."

They waited.

"He didn't get it. He said he tried to read it, and it was complete gibberish. But he couldn't have tried that hard, could he? I mean, you guys saw how he was yesterday. He kept looking at me like I was crazy and he didn't even seem to want to listen. If he'd really tried, he'd have been able to understand it. I mean, I figured it out, and he's probably smarter than me. We've been doing all the same things since kindergarten. He's just being intentionally stupid about this. Anyway, I think he realized that I was thinking that, and he started getting all ticked off. He said a bunch of stuff...that I was a jerk if I thought this was a funny joke. But when I tried to say again that I wasn't playing around and told him a little bit about what's happened, he just got more insulting, saying that if I really believe all that stuff I must be losing touch with reality, that I've read too many sci-fi books, that you guys...well, you get the idea. It was pretty nasty. I was so mad that I couldn't even say anything, so he left the book and took off. I've thought of a few things to say to him since then, though."

"I'm sorry," Eve said. "That sucks."

"It's weird that he would get that upset about it," said Alex. "I know it's hard to believe all this, but even if you were making it up, it's not really worth freaking out about, is it?"

Adam nodded. "That's the thing. It totally surprised me. I just figured that if he had time, he'd see what we all saw. I guess I'm a moron. But even so, it's not like him to act like that. He's usually pretty laid-back about things. I've never seen him yell like he did today."

"Well, maybe it's like we were saying before, and you can't understand the book unless it was sent to you," suggested Alex.

"Maybe," Adam was looking glum. "I guess I didn't want to believe that because…well, it just makes the whole question of who sent the books all the weirder, you know? I mean, who could possibly know who would and wouldn't be able to understand the book? It would have to be someone who knows all of us, and that doesn't seem possible. No, to me it seems more likely that James is just being dense for some reason. I just can't figure out why."

"He was scared. Yesterday, at your house, he was really bothered by seeing all of us there with you like we'd known you forever."

Everyone turned to stare at Logan. He didn't look up from the grass he was picking apart.

112

"That would make sense," said Alex. "You could tell he was surprised when we showed up. If he was jealous, he wouldn't really want to believe that all this stuff that's happened was real, would he?"

"But he doesn't need to be jealous of you," protested Adam. "It's not like you guys wouldn't like him or like I'd be any less friends with him just because I hang out with you."

"No, but he's been your best friend forever, and now all of a sudden you have these other friends who are in on something that he's not even a part of. Anyone would feel a little worried."

Adam nodded and shrugged at the same time. "I guess."

Eve was still watching Logan. That had been pretty perceptive of him to figure out what was bothering James. Logan was a strange kid. He didn't say much, but she'd seen the way he watched everything so closely. Apparently he was seeing stuff that other people missed. She sure hadn't picked up on James being scared. She had just figured that anyone would have a hard time buying a story like the one Adam had told him.

Logan glanced up, saw her looking at him, and ducked his head again. He definitely didn't like attention, which, as far as Eve was concerned, was the weirdest thing about him.

"Did you?" asked Adam.

"Huh? Did I what?" Eve realized that the conversation had moved on while she'd been in her own world.

"Did you get the room reserved?"

"Oh, yeah, no problem. Six o-clock on Saturday night. We have to set up the chairs ourselves and put everything back when we're done."

"Did they ask you what it was for?" asked Alex.

"You just have to fill out this reservation sheet, and under 'Purpose' I put *book club*," Eve smiled. "Close enough, right?"

"Great," said Adam. He was being very business-like again, clearly wanting to move on from the James issue. "Do you have the flyer, Logan?"

Logan started to pull a notepad out of his backpack, but Alex stopped him.

"Wait. I think there's someone here."

They all looked around.

"I don't see anyone," said Eve.

But Alex was shaking her head. "Someone is watching us."

"But..." Eve began, but Adam silenced her with a wave.

He slowly walked around the entire circle, looking up in the branches and behind each tree trunk. Eventually he came back to where they were standing. He shook his head apologetically, "Sorry, Alex, but I don't see anyone."

"I know," she said. "But... I'm sure there's something...I don't know. Can we maybe go somewhere else to talk about this? Maybe your house, Eve?"

Eve thought that was taking it a little too far. It's one thing to have a creepy feeling or want to be cautious, but it was another thing to want to hang out at her house when her mother was home. *You think someone's watching us here, Alex? You haven't met Snoopy Spymaster at my house.*

Out loud she said, "We can if you really want, but there's no one here but us. And it's not like we're telling any big secrets."

Eve had been able to keep things offhand when she introduced the other kids that first day, but there had already been one interrogation since then about why she was spending so much time with these new friends. Eve was pretty good at deflecting questions with a well-designed alibi.

115

But if they were all in her house, her mom would not be able to resist trying to find out more about them and what they were doing. That could be disastrous if anything like the truth came out. Eve saw a string of little white pills and child-friendly therapists in her future.

"I know," said Alex. "But we really need to talk somewhere else."

"Why is this…"

"Listen," Adam interrupted her. "If Alex has a feeling about this, we should listen to her. Remember what happened when I went after the sword. It's better to be safe than sorry."

Sorry about what? thought Eve, but she didn't make any more objections. Her house was only about three blocks away, and there was no good reason for refusing to go there that didn't make her sound like a spoiled brat. They had traded basic information about their families, but no one had gone into much detail, so there was no way for anyone to know what they were dealing with when it came to her mom. *Oh well*, she internally shrugged. It's not like this would be the first time she had to talk her way around her mom. And hey, maybe she'd get lucky and her mom would be out running errands or something.

* * * * *

Eve didn't get lucky.

Not only was her mom home, but she was out front, watering her roses (perfect nozzle set to the perfect spray at the perfect distance) and watching them as they walked up the street.

"Well, hello there," she said in a cheery voice that didn't deceive Eve a bit. "I thought you kids were going to be rehearsing again this morning."

"We are," said Eve, hoping desperately that none of the other kids felt the need to speak up, "but Adam's mom wasn't going to be home, so we decided to come over here and do it. We'll just be in my room and won't bother anyone."

"Of course you won't! But you don't need to hide away, either. I'd enjoy watching you work on your little play."

"Come on, Mom, we don't really want an audience yet."

"I don't think I really count as an audience."

"You would if you were watching us."

Eve saw that dangerous flicker in her mom's eyes at the tone of her voice, but she was still keeping the kind, motherly smile in place for the benefit of the other kids.

"I'd be real quiet, you know."

"It's just that some of us are kind of shy, Mrs. Sloane," said Adam suddenly. "We might be too self-conscious to make much progress with someone watching, until we're more ready, you know?"

Eve didn't think she'd ever been so surprised and grateful at the same time.

"Of course, dear, of course." Her mom looked like a dog who had been denied a bone. "I won't tease any more. You kids just run upstairs then. But wouldn't you like some lemonade or snacks or something before you get started?"

"No, thank you," they all repeated.

"All right then, but you take a break after awhile and we'll reconsider the snacks, okay?"

With a few mumbled assents, they finally made their escape. In Eve's room, the others immediately turned to her, questions on their faces. Well, this was inevitable. Anyway, it wasn't like she was the first person who ever lied to her mother. Once they got to know her, they'd understand perfectly. The sweet friendly mom act wouldn't hold up for five seconds if she knew what they were doing.

"So what exactly are we supposed to be rehearsing?" asked Adam.

"I know, I know, right? But after I introduced you guys that first day and we went to see the Gylf, she wouldn't let up with the questions. How did I meet you guys, who you were, and what we were doing all day. I tried to be vague, but once she's onto something, she can be relentless. I think...okay it's a little embarrassing, but we are boy-girl, boy-girl, you know? I think she was worried it was some sort of dating thing. Anyway, I knew I was going to have to come up with something good, and the truth was clearly not going to fly. I told you how she reacted to the book in the first place, and if I told her the rest she'd probably have me locked up or something. She's not exactly what you'd call open-minded." Eve realized that she was talking too much and too fast, so she took a deep breath. "So, yeah, I told her that you guys had been in the drama groups in middle school and that there was a special play that Mrs. Harris (she's the drama teacher at Dunmore High) wanted the four of us to do at the start of school and we'd be rehearsing it this summer. I know it sounds lame, but it had to be something that would explain why I didn't really know anything about you guys, but we were still going to spend so much time together. Anyway, thanks for not blowing my cover."

"It's all right," shrugged Adam. "I know how it is. My mom can be a head case sometimes, too."

Eve was relieved that no one was going to get self-righteous about it. She hadn't realized until now how much she wanted them to think well of her, and she hated the sound of the nervous giggle that came out of her mouth. "You can be glad you don't have a mom to worry about, Alex."

As soon as she said it, she realized what an awful thing it was to say. "Oh Alex, I'm sorry. I didn't…"

"I know," Alex stopped her. "I know you didn't mean that. But for the record, it's not true. A crazy mom is a lot better than no mom at all."

"Of course…I have no idea why I said that. I'm a complete jerk."

"You must really miss your mom," said Logan in that way he had.

"Yes. At least I miss having a mom. The truth is that I only have a few memories of her. I was only four when she died."

"That's so young…it must have been so hard for you," said Eve.

"At the time it wasn't that bad. I mean, I was so little I didn't really understand what had happened. All I can remember of the time around the funeral is that people kept giving me candy. I think I actually thought it was kind of fun. It wasn't until later that I missed my mom. When she wasn't there to play games with me. When a little girl in kindergarten made fun of the tangles in my hair that my dad didn't think to comb out. When all the other kids were buying school clothes with their moms or having their moms pack their lunches with healthy food. I would trade my Twinkies for their apples, and I know they thought I was crazy. But I always thought they were lucky to have someone who worried about that sort of thing. My dad is awesome, but there are a lot of things that dads just don't think of, you know? I think it was even harder for him than it was for me. But he always tried to make things fun for me. He still does."

Must be nice, thought Eve, but not wanting to stick her foot in her mouth again, she didn't say anything.

"I thought about telling him about the book actually," Alex went on. "But I decided against it for now. I may tell him later when we know more. He'll be lost to the world until he finishes his next edition anyway. Would you guys ever say anything to your parents?"

"No way," said Adam. "I'm with Eve. Mine are not the understanding type."

Logan absently ran his thumb over the cover of the sketchpad that he had taken from his backpack. "I don't know. My mom is gone at work most of the time, and when she's home she's so tired; I can't really picture myself having

121

this conversation with her. But if I ever needed to for some reason, I don't think she'd freak out or anything. I don't know if she'd believe it, but... she surprises me sometimes."

After a brief pause, Adam brought them back to the matter at hand, and they looked at the flyers that Logan had drawn up. He'd made a few different styles, but it only took one look for everyone to cast their vote. It was a simple layout with the symbol from the Redoubt, a circle within a circle within a circle. Underneath he had written the date and time and place of the meeting and the single phrase in large lettering: *gendel sea.*

Chapter 10

An Invisible Hand

The pounding on the door brought Alex awake with a jerk. For two dark seconds, she thought she'd gone blind, but then the digital numbers on her clock swam into focus: 5:03. She wasn't blind; it was still night.

More pounding. Who would be here at this hour?

The bathroom across the hall had a window that looked out on the front lawn. She quickly pulled away the blinds and looked down. It was Adam, and he was looking around anxiously. Alex's initial confusion was instantly drowned by fear.

Pulling a sweatshirt over her head, she sprinted for the door and yanked it open just as he was about to start pounding again. He stopped short so quickly he almost fell over.

"What are you doing?"

"I'm sorry, I need to see your book. Do you have your book?"

"What?"

"The Book of Sight. I need to see it."

"You're pounding on my door at five in the morning for that? What's wrong with your own book? Or your phone?"

"Can I come inside?"

Without replying, she stood back and let him in.

"I'm sorry I was so loud. I hope I didn't wake your dad up."

"No, he's sleeping out back. He sleeps like the dead anyway."

"Good. I mean, I'm glad I didn't bother him. I just had to see your book for myself. To make sure."

"To make sure of what? What's wrong with you?"

"My book is gone."

It was a simple enough statement, but it failed to connect in Alex's brain.

"What?"

"My book is gone. Remember how I said yesterday that I left it at home on the table? Well, it wasn't there when I got home last night. I figured it was no big deal, maybe I left it someplace else or my mom put it in my room when she was picking up. But it wasn't in my room, either. I looked everywhere, and I can't find it."

"Well, if your mom moved it, maybe she just put it somewhere else."

"I asked her. She says she didn't clean the house yesterday and she didn't see any book on the table. And I searched the whole house, not just my room."

"Yeah, but sometimes you just overlook something. My dad loses his keys pretty much every time he uses them, and we've turned the house upside down until we give up only to discover them in a pile of newspapers the next morning when we aren't even looking."

"I know," Adam nodded. "I know…but that book is a lot bigger than a set of keys. And I'm telling you, it's just not there."

"Are you sure that James didn't take it back when he left?"

Adam's lip curled. "I'm sure. He didn't want anything to do with it, remember? Besides, I distinctly remember that I thought about throwing it at his head as he was closing the door. No, it was there when I left and gone when I came home last night."

"So what are you saying? That someone stole it?"

"I don't know. I mean, maybe you're right. Maybe it's just misplaced and I missed it when I was looking. That's what I figured when I went to bed. But I couldn't sleep. And then all of a sudden I thought about what the Dund told us those men had said: 'We have to get back what he took from us.' What if someone stole the book from them? What if that same person stole my book? All of a sudden I was totally freaked out, and I had to come over and see if yours was still here."

Alex's backpack was on the dining room table where she'd slung it when she got home from a long afternoon of hanging up flyers. Even though she knew the book was inside, she found that she was fumbling with the zipper in her haste to open it.

The book was there.

She held it out to Adam, and he let out a sigh.

The ornately traced red cover felt good in her hands. Safe. Alex knew that it was only logical to think that Adam had simply misplaced his book, but something inside her was saying that the instinct that brought him over here at five in the morning was truer than logic. It was the same little voice that had told her they were being watched yesterday morning.

That thought clicked something into place.

"You said it was sitting on the table."

"Yeah, but it's not there, trust me, I looked..." he broke off at the look on her face. "What?"

"There was someone watching us. I know it. And they would have heard you say that."

"Oh...no way...I didn't even think of that." Adam's face was a study of combined awe and anger. "Who would do that?"

"I don't know. I really don't. But think about it...a book that can make you see things that no one else sees? That's a really big deal. There's obviously someone who wants people to have it and use it, someone who sent it to us. But maybe there is also someone who doesn't want people to have it."

"And that person must be pretty good at keeping it a secret because no one knows about it."

Alex felt a tingle of fear run up her spine. "So they find out who received the books and steal them? And they must know about the Redoubt because they knew to spy on us there."

"But how were they spying? There wasn't anyone there."

"No one that we could see. But, come on, after all we've seen and done in the last couple of weeks, it's not that hard to imagine there being someone there that was...invisible or something."

"Someone...or some thing."

Alex shivered.

"So what are we supposed to do?" asked Adam. "We know the Redoubt probably isn't safe any more, but we don't have any idea why. I mean," he ran a frustrated hand through his hair, making bits of it stand on end, "we don't even know who *sent* us the books much less who might want to steal them."

"*Gendel sea*," said Alex. "We just keep going on. We have the meeting tomorrow night, or tonight I guess it is now, and we see who comes. Then we take it from there. None of us asked to have the book sent to us. But it was, and I'm glad. You are, too, right? Whatever this is, it's huge, and I wouldn't want to never know about it."

"You're right. Obviously." Adam gave her a half smile. "But I sure hope someone comes to this meeting. Someone who knows something, 'cause not knowing anything is really starting to get to me. I wonder why the person who sent the books couldn't just send a letter with it, a note, anything. I mean, would it have killed them to write their name and a return address?"

"Maybe it would have," said Alex quietly.

Adam looked like he couldn't tell if she was joking or not.

She wasn't.

He laughed nervously. "I am really hoping that this is not that serious. And did you ever think that we don't even know who the good guys are? I mean, what if the person sending out the books is the bad guy and the other ones are trying to save us?"

"They aren't."

"But how do you know that?"

"I just do." Alex held up the book. "This is good. I think we all know that. Anyone who is trying to keep it a secret is trying to cover up something really good."

Adam was silent, but Alex knew he agreed with her. He reached out a finger and touched the red cover in her hands.

"Can I see this for a minute?" He thumbed through the pages. "I want to see if it says *gendel sea* in any of the other stories. I thought of that earlier. That was what first made me look for my book tonight before bed. Yes! Here it is in the second chapter. It's repeated several times."

Alex looked over his shoulder and began to read. Began to *read* the words on the page he had pointed out.

The story made sense.

Hot and cold chills passed over her body.

Adam let out his breath in a hiss.

"Can you understand it?"

"Yes. You?"

"Yes."

He turned back two pages to where the second chapter started. Fifty times Alex had tried to read this page and it had always remained a stubborn sequence of nonsense words and random letters. But she could tell before she even started that this time was going to be different. The words seemed to jump off the page at her, waving as if greeting an old friend, and beckoning her in to where the beautiful pictures would fill her mind. For just a second, she raised her head and caught Adam's eye. He gave a tiny nod, and they both turned and lost themselves to the story.

This time Alex found herself looking out through the eyes of a young man, a prince...

She felt his agony as he heard of the betrayal of his brother, his guilt over his part in pushing his brother to such an extremity. She tasted his disgust on her lips as he spoke the necessary words of banishment and smiled in grim satisfaction as she made arrangements to follow her brother into exile. If her brother must be lost, she would go with him, protect him, redeem him if she could. It seemed to Alex that she lived years of wanderings, of dangers, of discomfort, but also of fleeting joys and chance meetings of hope. She followed her brother's aimless path and did what she could to repay his debts, repair that which he broke, give aid to those he turned away. And each place she went, she left behind a token, an eagle carved by hand from bits of wood in remembrance of her family crest. At times, she lost hope, but always there was someone who came with the right words. Gendel sea. She carried on. Time and time again her brother sought his own destruction in bad company and evil living, and time and time again she was able to save him at the final moment. Until one day she could not. She arrived too late, her brother already falling before her eyes at the hand of his own ill companions. Her years of sacrifice in vain, Alex despaired utterly. She charged her brother's attackers in blind rage, only to find herself overpowered. Soon she was facing her own death, accepting the cold clear-headedness that came with it, conscious only of a sense of loss, of life wasted, of noble purpose thwarted by petty ugliness. Her point of view shifted. She rose above the young man's lifeless body, watching as the brigands left him and he was carried by some peasants to the top of the hill. Men and women came from miles around to lay tiny carved eagles on his grave, raising a mound high enough to be seen from the valley below, a wordless epitaph silhouetted against the sky.

Chapter 11

Gendel Sea

Adam had a brother, but he had never felt much of a brotherly bond. Living in the same house for fifteen years had given them a lot of the same memories, but it hadn't made them understand each other.

Adam's brother, Brian, was only two years older but those two years might as well have been twenty for all that they had in common. Brian's world was balls and bats, nightly sports broadcasts, and a string of beautiful but boring girlfriends.

Adam's world wasn't even in the same universe. It was peopled mostly by the characters from the books he read, along with James and handful of other friends. As far as Adam could tell, Brian barely knew he existed, and Adam told himself he was just fine with that.

In James, Adam had a friend that shared all of his interests. They'd known each other forever.

They had discovered the Hardy Boys at the same time, had staged elaborate mock battles with their Star Wars action figures, and had camped out all night in each other's back yards. Adam knew James's top five movie moments, and James knew which of Piers Anthony's novels was Adam's favorite. They'd been using the words "best friend" since first grade, and it was an accurate description. Until this week, they'd never had a fight that was worth the name. If you had asked Adam before, he would have said that James was like a brother to him and he would have meant it.

But that morning, sitting with Alex and Logan and Eve in the empty field where the Dund lived and reading together the second chapter of the Book of Sight, Adam felt like he understood the word brother for the first time. More than living near each other or sharing interests, being brothers was about having a shared identity. Adam hadn't even known that was possible. Something had happened to each of them in these last weeks, and even though they had little in common, they were now all something different from everyone else. The weird thing was that Adam didn't even know what that thing was. He just knew they were in it together.

He and Alex had read the second chapter in what seemed like only minutes. Though neither was reading out loud, they both finished at the same moment and dropped the book in one shared motion. Adam's mind was reeling, sorting through the flurry of emotions created by the story he'd just read, but on top of all that was a single urgent thought. *We have to show this to the others.* Somehow he knew that Alex was thinking the same thing.

They had gone straight to Eve's house. Adam had waited on the sidewalk while Alex tossed pieces of bark dust at Eve's window. Eve finally appeared and was surprisingly eager to grab her book and climb down. It was clear that this wasn't her first escape from the window. Alex hadn't even needed to offer much explanation.

The sun was barely coming up when they arrived at Logan's trailer. No car was in the driveway, so they knew his mom hadn't arrived home from her graveyard shift at the shoe factory. A few taps on the metal door brought Logan out, looking surprised and sleepy. When they told them why they'd come, the fog lifted immediately and he scrambled to find his copy of the book. Logan led them to a corner of the empty field where no one would bother them but where he could still see the trailer that held his sleeping little brother and sister. Then, sitting closely together, they opened all three books and, Adam looking over Alex's shoulder, began to read. Adam heard Logan sigh and Eve gasp, and then he was lost again in the wonderful words before him.

Once again, they all arrived at the end at the same time, and there was a universal shifting as they came back to themselves. Adam stretched and looked around.

One glance at Logan's face and Adam could see how deep the emotions went. He was pretty sure there were tears in Logan's eyes. Out of common decency, he looked away.

Instead, he focused on Eve and felt the last of his dislike for her (which had been slowly fading away anyway) disappear forever. She was glowing with a sort of internal radiance that made him feel like she might burst into flames right there on the spot. In a word, she was beautiful. Then she opened her mouth, and he thought she would ruin the moment with her usual thoughtless babble. But she didn't. She laughed. Just exactly the sort of joyous and unplanned laughter that perfectly expressed how he felt. How could he have ever thought she was a hopeless waste? He wouldn't have thought it possible, but this girl *got* it.

Alex began to laugh along with her, and Adam saw that there were tears in her eyes, too. Soon they were all laughing, and that's when Adam knew. He knew that whatever it was that they all were now, it was never going to go away.

* * * * *

By the time they were gathered later in the slightly musty smelling classroom in the library basement, their euphoria had settled down some. Adam could still feel the buzz of adrenalin coursing through his system, and judging from the way the others were fidgeting, he guessed they were feeling the same way. But at least they were calm enough to talk about things.

The posters had advertised the meeting for 6:00, and as they talked Adam couldn't keep himself from watching the clock and wondering. He didn't want to think about how much he was counting on someone coming tonight.

"So I tried to reread the story this afternoon," said Eve.

"And?"

"Nope, it didn't make sense. I mean, I remembered the story and could imagine it, but only as much as I could picture it without even looking at the book. Reading it was impossible."

"I told you," said Adam. (*5:55. It was too much to hope that anyone would come early, but that didn't mean they weren't coming.*) "We can only read it when we're together. I'll bet you anything."

"I know," said Eve, "but I couldn't help wanting to find out for sure. You know me...or I mean, I guess you really don't know me that well, but you could probably figure out by now that I have to learn things the hard way."

"Did you guys have any luck finding Adam's book?" Alex asked.

Adam just shook his head. That was one topic he didn't feel like talking about.

"Someone has to have taken it," Logan said. "We tore that place apart this afternoon, and it's not anywhere. And everyone in Adam's family says they haven't seen it."

"Well, we pretty much knew it was stolen, but I guess it's always better to make sure," said Alex.

"I'm really sorry, Adam," Eve said. "It must suck like crazy not to have your book, especially right now."

"Yeah," and then realizing how rude that sounded, he added, "But as you were so happy to test for us, we can't read the second story unless we're together anyway, so sharing isn't that big of a deal."

It felt like a big deal, though...a really big deal. Rational or not, he couldn't help feeling like the Book of Sight was a valuable treasure that had been entrusted to him. And he had failed in that trust.

Seriously though, he thought angrily in the general direction of whoever had sent that book, *couldn't you have just enclosed a little note letting us know that someone would be coming along wanting to steal the freaking thing? Some warning would have helped.*

"Well, at least now the rest of us know that we have to keep our books close. And we may still find out who took yours and have a chance to get it back," said Alex.

Adam nodded. (*6:00. Still no one.*) A longer than normal lull in conversation told Adam that he wasn't the only one watching the clock.

After a few minutes, Logan spoke up, "Now that we know there's a thief, we may be able to catch him in the act. Adam and I talked about this a little bit this afternoon. Whoever it is, we're assuming they'll want to steal the other books, too. But if we were waiting for it, we could catch them. Or follow them. Or at least we'd see who it is."

"You mean use the books as bait," said Alex.

"I think that's the plan that they always use in the movies, and then something goes seriously wrong," Eve said.

"Well, maybe someone will come who knows something and then we won't have to worry about it," said Adam, but he was thinking, *6:05...6:06...no one's coming.*

"I sure hope so," said Eve. "I don't know about you guys, but I'm starting to feel like I *have* to know what's up with this book. The last couple of weeks have been one crazy new thing after another, and it doesn't seem like it's going to stop. I want to know what's going on."

"But good crazy," Logan said.

"Definitely," agreed Alex.

"So are we ever going to talk about the second story?" asked Eve after a pause.

"What's there to say?" responded Alex.

"Well, didn't it seem to you that…" Adam broke off. *6:13. Was that someone in the hall?*

The door opened and a boy walked in. He stopped abruptly when he saw them, as if he was surprised to see them there. For a second Adam thought the new kid was going to just turn around and walk out without saying anything, but before he could, Eve stepped forward.

"Are you here for the meeting?" She held up one of the flyers they had posted around town.

The boy nodded slowly, glancing around the room as if looking for someone else to be there besides the four kids in front of him. Adam thought this kid couldn't be too much older than they were, but he didn't remember ever seeing him before. He was tall and had longish dark hair and brown skin. A Mexican, maybe? Most of the Mexicans lived south of town and didn't mix much with everyone else. But where he came from wasn't the question here.

"So you got the book, too?" asked Adam.

"Book?"

"Yeah," Adam held up Alex's copy. "We all have it."

"Oh, sorry," the kid looked embarrassed. "Is this some kind of book club? I didn't know." He looked toward the door like he was wishing he'd never walked through it.

Adam was shaken. "No, it's...you mean you haven't read this book?"

The kid shook his head.

For a second no one said anything. Adam couldn't think what to say. He should have realized that this could happen, that someone would just see the posters and come out of curiosity. It was stupid to feel so disappointed about it.

"But how did you recognize the signs if you haven't read the book?" asked Logan, and seeing the boys surprised glance, "*Gendel Sea.* You came because you recognized the words." It wasn't a question.

"Yeah," said the kid. "Um, those words are on a painting my grandmother has in her house."

Adam smiled. His previous doubts melted in the sudden flame of excitement in his chest.

"How did you know about the words?" The kid was studying Logan with a hint of something in his eyes that could have been suspicion.

Logan shrugged. "I just saw how you looked at the flyer when Eve showed it to you. I'm Logan, by the way."

"Dominic."

Adam stepped forward. "And I'm Adam. This is Alex and Eve. You said that your grandmother has a painting with the words *gendel sea*?"

"Yeah, she's had it hanging in the upstairs hall for as long as I can remember."

"What's it like?"

The boy shrugged. "It's just this guy holding up a torch and looking down into a dark cave. And on the frame there's a little metal thing with the words carved in it."

"And when you saw the flyers for the meeting you remembered the painting."

"Yeah, I always liked that painting." As soon as he said it, he looked embarrassed, but he didn't drop his eyes.

"Do you know what *gendel sea* means, then?" asked Alex.

"No, I figured maybe whatever this meeting was might explain more about it. That's

141

why I came. Though I sort of figured I could just sneak in the back and listen for a while."

"Instead here we were waiting for you," said Eve. "Did your grandmother ever say where she got the painting?"

"I think she brought it with her from Mexico when she married my grandfather."

"But she didn't tell you what it means? Is it Spanish?" Adam asked.

"No, it's not Spanish. When I asked her about it when I was little, she just shrugged." Dominic looked around at them all. "But don't you guys know what it means? You wrote it on flyers and put them up all over town."

This made them all pause and look at each other. Finally Alex said, "We *think* we know what it means. It's a really important part of this book."

Dominic looked at them expectantly, but no one said anything, so finally he came out and asked, "So, what does it mean?"

Each of them paused, waiting for someone else to answer, and then when it seemed that no one else would, they all answered at the same time.

"Together," said Eve.

"Courage," said Adam.

"Light," said Logan.

Only Alex didn't say anything.

Dominic raised one eyebrow. "It sounds like you don't quite agree about what it means."

Adam immediately felt defensive, but before he could think of a good response, Alex spoke up.

"It means all of those things, and... and more. You can't put it into words. You just feel it. That's the way the stuff in the book is. You don't understand because you haven't read it."

Dominic accepted this without responding.

"So I guess the obvious question is if you want to read it now," said Eve. "So far no one we've talked to has been very...um...interested in reading the book. But then, none of them would have come here tonight, either."

"I'm interested," Dominic said, and Eve handed him the book.

They all waited, watching with great interest as he began to read the first page. Adam didn't know if he was more expecting this kid to stop after the first few nonsense words as James had done or to make them wait an hour as he lost himself in the story. As it turned out, neither of those things happened.

Dominic read the first two pages and then looked up in surprise, "I know this story. My grandmother used to tell it to me at bedtime when I was little. This is a lot more... you know...but it's definitely the same story."

A huge smile lit Adam's face. He couldn't help it. He could feel some answers on their way.

Maybe this Dominic kid didn't know too much, but the grandmother obviously knew something.

"So you didn't have any trouble understanding it?" Alex asked.

"No, I recognized it right away."

They looked at each other with a mixture of amazement and excitement.

"And, um, have you ever seen anything that you would say really shouldn't be there?" asked Adam.

"What do you mean?"

"Just things that you can see that maybe no one else can see," explained Eve.

A hard, closed look came into Dominic's dark eyes. "Maybe."

"So maybe it isn't just the book. Maybe it's the stories," said Adam to the others.

"What are you guys talking about?" asked Dominic, that suspicious tone back in his voice.

"We have a story to tell you that might be interesting to you," said Alex.

"And maybe you can help us figure out what comes next," added Adam.

Chapter 12

Distant and Alive

Everyone was already at Alex's house when Dominic showed up the next day. They had agreed to meet at ten, and Alex knew he would come, to return her book if nothing else. She got the distinct feeling that this was a guy who always showed up when he said he would.

He did, though not until he was late enough to make Adam start asking nervous questions. Dominic's face was impassive, but the look in his eyes said clearly that he had read the first chapter. Without anyone needing to say anything, they knew he was one of them now.

Not that a lack of need was going to hinder Adam from saying something. Or Eve, for that matter.

"You read it?" asked Adam.

"Yeah."

"And what did you think?"

Dominic shrugged. "It was my grandmother's story. But, you know…"

"And did you read the second one, too?" Eve asked.

"It didn't make any sense. None of the other stories did." And when they all shared a knowing look. "What? Is there something you didn't tell me?"

"We just wanted to see if it would be the same with you," Alex explained. "We have only been able to read the first two stories. But the second one we can only read when we're together."

"You mean you read it to each other?"

"Not necessarily. We just have to be with each other when we're reading it or else we don't understand the words."

Dominic gave her a skeptical look that made Alex briefly wish she had the Mist's flame throwing ability, but then he shrugged and took out the book. Flipping to the second chapter he began to read. Two lines in, he glanced up in surprise. Alex smiled as he dropped his head again and kept on reading.

Adam flashed Alex a conspiratorial grin and picked up Eve's book off the bed. Very quietly, Logan took his book out, too, and they all began to read.

Dominic finished first. Alex heard his book snap shut, but she didn't stop reading until she came to the end of the story. When she finally looked up, she saw that he was staring out the window, dry-eyed and motionless. Adam caught her eye again with a questioning look. Alex shrugged.

"I could read that a thousand times and never get tired of it," Eve's voice broke in. Dominic seemed to come back from far away.

"Believe us now?" Alex couldn't help but ask.

"It's the weirdest thing I've ever seen," said Dominic.

"Yeah, tell us about it," said Adam. "We were hoping maybe your grandmother would know something about all this. Did you tell her about the book?"

"She was asleep when I got home last night and in her garden when I left this morning. But I really don't think she has seen a book like this. She told me that story was one her father used to tell her."

"Still," said Adam. "It's worth asking, isn't it? If she knows anything at all, that'll be more than we know now. All this weird stuff keeps happening to us, but we don't seem to get any closer to figuring out how or why."

Dominic nodded. "We can go and talk to her. But like I said, I'm pretty sure that she hasn't read this book. She doesn't even speak much English."

"Well, this book isn't exactly English, is it?" said Eve. "As the Dund would say, 'You never know until you try.'"

* * * * *

The house where Dominic lived with his grandparents was in the foothills outside of town. It was made from adobe and was obviously very old, but an inviting wooden porch looked over a beautiful garden surrounded by a homemade wooden fence.

Dominic's grandmother was in the garden, using a hoe to dig weeds out from around a row of perfect rose bushes. She was a little woman with long white hair in a braid down her back and a slight curve to her spine, but she wielded the hoe with as much energy as Alex could have done. On the porch, an old man with the most wrinkled brown skin Alex had ever seen was asleep in a rocking chair.

The old woman in the garden looked up as they approached and leaned on her hoe, smiling widely. "*Dominico, mijo. Trajiste unos amigos.*"

Dominic leaned down and kissed her on the cheek. "*Si, abuela. Son unos chicos que conocí ayer. Le presento a Adam y a Alex y a Eve y a Logan.*" They all smiled at the mention of their names. "Guys, this is my abuela. *Abue, tenemos unas preguntas para usted.*"

"*Preguntas para mi? Que tiene una vieja como yo que interesa a los jovenes?*"

"*Tiene que ver con el cuento que siempre me contabas cuando era niño, lo del rey y el círculo de arboles. Ellos tienen un libro con ese cuento."*

"En serio? Un libro? Entonces no hace falta que yo cuente la historia. No sé que mas tengo para ayudarlos. Pero contesto todas las preguntas que tienen...si puedo. Vamos adentro. Si no tengo respuestas, por lo menos tengo galletas y limonada."

She turned and began to hobble quickly into the house.

"She says to come inside," said Dominic. "She has cookies and lemonade, but she doesn't think she knows anything that will help you."

Us, thought Alex. *You mean that she doesn't know anything that will help us. You're a part of this, too, you know, whether you like it or not.*

Inside the big kitchen, they all took seats around the wooden table while Dominic's grandmother quickly poured tall glasses of lemonade and set out a plate of sugar cookies. They each smiled and thanked her as she handed the glasses around. Finally, when Dominic convinced her that they were all comfortable and had everything they needed, she sat down. Her own glass held plain water.

"Ahora, que quieren saber de esta viejita?"

"She's ready for your questions," translated Dominic.

After a moment's awkward pause, Adam spoke up. "We mostly want to know if she's ever seen a book like this before." He slid it across the table.

The old woman picked up the book in her gnarled hands and felt the soft leather cover. "*Es lindo. Un libro hermoso.*" She looked inside. "*Nunca vi un libro asi. No lo puedo leer. Esta en ingles?*"

"*No se, abue. Me parece que es otra idioma. Pero se puede leer un poquito igual.*"

She looked at it some more and then shook her head. "*No entiendo nada. Lo siento, no conozco este libro.*"

"She's never seen anything like it before. And she can't read it, either."

Alex could see how disappointed Adam was. She wasn't surprised, though. After all, Dominic had said his grandmother only heard the story from her father.

"The story you used to tell Dominic," she said. "You heard it from your father?"

Dominic translated and listened to her reply. "She says yes, that he told her the story when she was a little girl. She thinks he heard it from his father. It is a very old story."

"What about the painting?" asked Logan. "You said she has a painting with the words *gendel sea* on it."

Dominic asked his grandmother something in Spanish. She replied, and he got up and went up the stairs.

Left alone with the old *abuela*, the kids felt a little awkward. She began to offer around the plate of cookies again, urging them in her beautiful Spanish to eat more. Alex wasn't hungry, but the cookies were really good, so it wasn't much of a sacrifice to take another one.

In a moment, Dominic came back with the painting held in both hands. It was bigger than Alex expected and had what looked like a hand-carved wooden frame. When he turned it toward her, Alex sucked her breath in quickly. It was beautiful. The dark cave that gaped in front of the young man was terrifying, but his face showed no fear. The colors were exquisite and the light from the torch in the man's hand seemed to actually glow, but Alex couldn't take her eyes off the man's face. Why did it seem so familiar?

"Can you ask her where she got this painting?" breathed Adam.

After a short exchange in Spanish, Dominic looked surprised. He said nothing until Adam prompted him, "What did she say?"

"She said this one isn't the one she brought from Mexico with her. She said my mother brought this one home not long before I was born."

There was a silence. Alex turned from the painting to look at Dominic, but she couldn't read anything in his face. None of them knew what had happened to Dominic's parents. He'd mentioned that first night that he lived with his grandparents but had never said anything about his mom or dad.

151

Alex could tell that no one knew what to say or do. But she hated how people always seemed afraid of offending her by mentioning her mother, so she decided to just be direct.

"Did your mother die?" she asked.

Adam looked down uncomfortably, but Alex kept her eyes fixed steadily on Dominic's face.

"No," he said. "She's still alive, but she's very sick. A couple of years ago, she started getting worse, so they sent her to live on my great-grandfather's farm in Mexico. I stayed here to be in school and help my grandparents."

"Do you get to talk to her often?" asked Alex.

"There's no phone in the village where she's at. Once a year she goes to the city to call me for my birthday. She writes me letters pretty often, though."

"I'm sorry," said Alex. "You must miss her."

"Yeah."

After another pause, Dominic leaned the painting against the wall. "So, you're no closer to understanding anything that you were when you came. Sorry."

"That's okay," said Eve. "You told us that would happen. And we did get some awesome cookies and lemonade. Gracias, Mrs. Valterra."

"Hernandez," said Dominic. "Valterra was my dad's name."

152

"Oh, right. Gracias, Mrs. Hernandez."

The little lady smiled as they all thanked her, and before anyone could protest, she'd taken another dozen cookies from the cupboard and wrapped them in paper. She handed these to Eve and shook her head firmly to indicate that she would not be refused. Alex left the cozy kitchen feeling like she'd just met the definition of the word "grandmother".

On the front porch, Adam looked around at everyone. "So where to now? Should we take Dominic to see the Gylf?"

"Actually," said Logan. "I think he has something to show us."

Dominic whirled around. "How did you know that?"

Logan shrugged. "You looked like you were trying to decide something. And you kept looking at that one spot off in the woods over there."

"Logan's a little bit psychic," said Adam.

Dominic smiled, but Alex thought he looked uncomfortable with the idea.

"So what do you have to show us?" asked Eve.

"Well, you asked if I'd ever seen anything that no one else could see." He was leading the way through the garden gate and toward the trees across the dirt road. "I found this when I was a little kid and I used to love to play here. But one time I showed it to a kid from school, and he said

153

it was just a bunch of tree roots. It's...well, you'll see."

Beyond the tree line, the ground dropped away sharply. Alex soon found herself half sliding down a leaf-covered embankment.

They all finally came crackling and crunching to a stop at the bottom, and Dominic led the way off to the left. About fifty feet from where they started, a huge tree blocked the way. Dominic skirted this and stopped on the other side. Alex was the last in line, so she heard the others' exclamations of wonder before she saw anything. Then she, too, rounded the tree and felt her heart constrict.

There in front of her was a tiny village. On this side, the giant tree's roots looped up out of the ground in weird natural formations. But these had been shaped and carved into small houses, and beyond the roots, the embankment was also full of tiny doorways and windows. There were smoothed places that must have been roads and broken down fences around what might have once been gardens. Whoever had lived here had been very small. The doorways were only about two feet tall. The occupants were obviously long gone though. Weeds had grown up over most of the fences and the houses in the embankment were beginning to crumble.

"It looks like something from a movie," said Eve. "Like hobbits are going to come out of those doors or something."

"Looks a little small for hobbits," said Adam absently.

154

Eve laughed. "Sorry I'm not up on my hobbit dimensions."

"So you found this years ago?" asked Logan.

Dominic nodded.

"And that kid you brought here couldn't see a village? That's crazy. You'd have to be blind to miss it," said Adam.

"That's pretty much what I thought," said Dominic. "But I never brought anyone else here anyway. Then last night you guys were talking about meeting little people in the woods and I thought maybe they were the same sort of people who made this place."

"I don't think so," said Alex. "These places would be a little too big for them, I think. Besides, their home didn't look anything like recognizable houses. They seem to like to...blend in more."

"Just because we recognize these as houses doesn't mean they're obvious to everyone," said Eve.

"True," Adam said. "But I agree with Alex. These don't feel like Gylf houses."

"So who did make them?" asked Logan.

Adam shrugged.

"I guess we can add that to our list of mysteries," said Dominic, and Alex noticed that he was including himself with them now. "I'm just glad you guys saw what I saw."

155

"This must have been an amazing place to play as a kid," Alex said.

"Yeah."

"Do you guys think there are places like this all over?" asked Eve. "I mean, not necessarily just like this...but, you know, places that no one notices...places that are like something from another world. Who knows what you'll find around the next corner and all that?"

"I'm starting to think there are," said Alex.

"Just look at all we've found since we first read the book, and it's only been a couple of weeks," Adam said.

"So even though it feels like we don't know anything at all, we're not totally in the dark. At least now we know how ignorant we were before," said Eve.

Alex hadn't thought of it that way, but she knew immediately that Eve was right. Whoever sent them those books wasn't trying to keep secrets from them. They were trying to reveal secrets. Just maybe not all at once.

"Hey guys, look at this," said Logan. He was kneeling in front of one of the doorways in the embankment, peering inside. Alex knelt next to him. It was very dark inside, but a small patch of light from a window fell on what must have been the wooden front door, now lying on the floor inside. And carved into the middle of the door was a symbol that Alex recognized immediately: a circle within a circle within a circle.

"I think the next place we need to show Dominic is the Redoubt," said Logan.

Chapter 13

Selling Rotten Fruit

When Logan woke the next morning, he had an instant feeling that something was wrong. In the first place, he wasn't in his own bed. But that wasn't anything unusual. Sam, his little brother, frequently had nightmares, and lying down next to him on his bed was the easiest way to calm him down.

So why did he have that nagging feeling of having left something important undone?

There was Sam next to him, fast asleep, and Darcy was snoring a little bit in the room she shared with their mom. Everything seemed exactly the way it always was.

He got up and shuffled down the cramped hall to the kitchen. The little clock on the microwave said 7:09. His mom would be coming home from work soon, tired out after another long graveyard shift. He'd better put on some water. She usually liked a cup of tea before falling into her bed.

Turning from the stove, his eyes fell on the door, and he realized that it was unlocked. Well, that explained the feeling of having forgotten something. How stupid could he be? He always locked that door, but he must have forgotten after his mom left last night. He had been a little off, getting home from the Redoubt just barely in time for her to leave. She'd been worried, and he had felt bad. Still, he thought he'd locked it, out of habit if nothing else.

Then an idea slammed into him like a freight train. He turned and stumbled back down to his bedroom. The pillow, he'd left it under the pillow. But it wasn't there. Dropping the pillow on the floor, he rifled through the sheets and blankets. Nothing. In desperation, he pulled the bed out from the wall and looked behind and under it. No book.

He took one calming breath and tried to think. Yes, he had definitely put the book under his pillow when he went to bed last night. They'd all agreed that was the thing to do, to make sure it was right there with them at all times. But then he'd been awakened by Sam's crying at 2:00 a.m. The book had been the furthest thing from his mind.

Still, in order to steal it, someone would have had to come right here into this room where both boys were sleeping and take it without either of them waking up. The thought of it made Logan turn cold. Someone, a stranger, opening the door, walking down the hall past a sleeping Darcy, entering the room, passing right next to him and Sam, maybe standing over them in the dark, feeling around in his bed and finding the book. And none of them had noticed anything. What if the thief had decided to do more than just steal the book? They'd all been sleeping and vulnerable.

Logan stopped himself. There was no point in imagining things after the fact. They were all fine. Only the book was missing. (Only the book, but already Logan was feeling its loss like an ache in his chest.)

He needed to be very sure. Slower this time, and methodically, Logan searched through his sheets and blankets and in and around the bed. He knew he wouldn't find it, but he forced himself to be thorough.

A shrill whistling sound finally put an end to his search. He headed back to the kitchen to make tea and prepare himself to break the bad news to the others.

* * * * *

They took it just as hard as he knew they would. Sitting in a loose circle in the Redoubt again, the faces all looked back at him bleakly. He was a little surprised (and lot relieved) that none of them showed any blame.

"But it was in the same room with you?" repeated Eve for the third time.

"Yeah."

"That is seriously disturbing."

Logan nodded and continued picking at the grass in front of him.

"We have to do something!" burst out Adam. "Whoever is doing this knows who we are and where we live. And if Alex is right, they were listening to us right here the other day. Maybe they're listening right now, and we wouldn't know because we can't see them."

"What about your idea of trying to lure the thief and then trap him?" said Eve.

Alex looked uncomfortable. "I really don't think we should be discussing this here. We are still being watched. I'm sure of it."

"Well, it may not be very secure here," said Adam. "But where are we going to go? I think we've already established that our houses aren't safe either."

"I know," insisted Alex, "but that doesn't mean we have to discuss secret strategies in a place where we know we're being spied on."

"Do we know it?" asked Dominic.

"Yes, we do," snapped Adam and Alex at the same time. Everyone saw Alex give Adam a look of gratitude, but Logan thought he might have been the only one who noticed the satisfaction on Adam's face when he received it.

"I'm just saying that feelings may or may not be accurate," said Dominic.

"Alex's are," Adam said with finality.

Dominic didn't respond, but his face said he wasn't convinced.

"Let's take another look around," suggested Logan. "We didn't see anything the last time, but I've heard that sometimes you can suddenly see things you didn't notice before."

The laughter at this broke the tension, and they all scattered around the circle, some studying the branches, some the ground.

After a minute, Eve gave a shrill whistle of excitement. "Hey, guys, look at this!" She was brushing away a tall stand of grass in the middle of the circle of trees, uncovering a small ring of flat stones embedded in the ground. But no one was looking at what she had found. Their attention had been attracted by something much more colorful.

As soon as Eve had whistled, something small and brilliantly pink had appeared in the branches over her head and then tumbled to the ground about two feet behind her. Adam and Logan remained frozen for a second, staring at the pink thing (Was it an animal?) on the ground. Alex stepped forward and opened her mouth, but before she could say anything, Dominic had darted across the circle and snatched it up in both hands. They all closed in to see what he had caught.

It was a lizard, very much like a little gecko, but with an abnormally large head. It must have had similar qualities to a chameleon because the hot pink color was already fading, and it was taking on the even brown tones of Dominic's hands. It wasn't struggling at all, but its eyes were darting in every direction. Logan

163

had no doubt that the moment it saw a chance to escape, it would take it.

"I think we've found our spy," said Dominic.

"Unless it's just a chameleon," Adam suggested, raising his eyebrows.

"What do you think?" Dominic held the creature up to Alex.

"He was listening," she said.

"You're saying that a little lizard carried off our books?" laughed Adam.

"No, but he could have told someone else where they were," she answered.

"We haven't seen any evidence that it can talk," Adam pointed out.

"So now you don't believe in Alex's feelings?" asked Dominic.

"So now you do?"

"Let's just see," said Dominic, and Logan could see that his hands had tightened. Now the creature did start to squirm.

"Don't hurt it!" cried Eve.

"I won't," Dominic said, "as long as it tells us what it's doing here and who it is reporting to."

Adam snorted, and Logan was tempted to laugh at the idea of interrogating a gecko, but something about the way the little head tilted to the side as if it understood…

"All right! Stop! Please stop! You caught me. I was listening. Just stop, stop, stop." The voice was louder and less shrill than you would have expected from something that small. "I'll talk. Talking is good. I have no problem talking. There's no need to squeeze. You win. You are very clever. You know all about me. You found me out. See, I'm talking. I'm cooperating. I'm a good little muxen."

The little creature said all this in the two seconds it took for Dominic to release the pressure. In fact, for a second Logan thought Dominic was going to drop the thing out of surprise. Apparently he hadn't been as confident that it would talk as he had seemed. They were all staring. Only Alex looked calm.

"What are you?" she asked.

"Of course that is the first question you would want to ask. Anyone would do the same I suppose. I'm not entirely sure that it's best for you to know, but I did say I would answer all your questions. You were clever enough to find me and quick enough to trap me and strong enough to…yes, yes, well to show good faith I will answer your question. I am Sarten, though most people call me only Sarty. I suppose you will do as most people do. That seems to be the way people like to act. So you'll call me Sarty. Though I hate that name. I should really much prefer Sarten. But that's of no matter. My name is not so very important. I'm really no one. It's not what you call me that matters. I'm just a little nobody, a little listener, so small, so insignificant. You really shouldn't mind me at all."

165

Now that he had started talking, he didn't seem to want to stop. His speech was clear, but so fast that Logan could barely understand it.

"But what *are* you, Sarten?"

"A muxen, of course. Don't tell me you don't know what a muxen is. The finest traders in gossip and information. If you haven't heard of us, you've been missing out. I have so much I could tell you. Just whatever you want to know."

"Okay," said Alex. "Why are you spying on us?"

"I wasn't spying on you. How could you say such a thing? No, not spying. Spying is such a nasty little word. I was listening. Just listening. Listening is what I do. And it's so harmless really. I just sit and bother no one and listen. And, oh, the things I learn. I know many things from just listening. Yes, there is always so much to listen to and so much to learn." A gleam came into his eye. "I love to listen. Oh, yes, I do. I am a listener, that's me. Just listening, listening, very small, very harmless, just a listener."

"Yes, but you didn't just listen," Alex interrupted. "You talked. You, um, 'traded' information about us. Who did you tell about us?"

"Who says I talked? Who told you such things about little Sarten? I didn't talk, oh no, not to anyone. I'd much rather listen and learn than talk. No, no, I most definitely didn't talk, so you see, you can let me go." It squealed as Dominic applied pressure again. "Okay, okay, I can see there is no fooling you. I said you were clever, and clever you are. You cannot be fooled. You can see that Sarten likes talking, too. Yes, half the fun of listening is telling what you've heard. And I've heard so many things in so many places. So much to tell, and he is a very interested listener. So I couldn't really help myself. It's the way I was made, you see. I listen and talk and talk and listen. And I have to talk to whoever will listen. And he is a very good listener. Oh yes, maybe not as good as Sarten, but a very good listener just the same."

"Who is?" asked Dominic.

"Oh, that's not important. You don't need to know that. Just listen to this…"

"Who is a good listener?"

"Oh, well, just him, you know. The one who told me to come back. Okay, I admit it, he told me to listen some more. Not that I minded. I liked listening. And this is a nice place to listen. And- ouch! Ouch! No need to squeeze! No need to hurt me! I'm talking. I'm talking all you want."

"Who did you talk to?" repeated Dominic over the little muxen's protests. "Just give us a name."

"I can't say! I can't see! I really can't say! You are clever. You will know that I'm telling the truth. I don't know his name. I don't really see him. Just hear him. Just listen and he asks and I tell and he is a very good listener. But he doesn't say much. No, he never said names. But I really think you worry too much about names. His name is not interesting. His name is not fun. I could tell you so many more interesting things, don't you know. I listen. I listen all over and I hear things. Did you know the farmer's creek is drying up? The creek, that lovely place, is all drying up, and the farmer says that it's a bad sign. That there isn't enough water. That there won't be good crops. He is very upset about his dried up creek. I can see that doesn't interest you. Okay, okay, I can understand that. The troubles of farmers aren't the most exciting news. But listen to this. The Hendersons...you know the Hendersons? Such a lovely family and such a beautiful house surrounded by trees. (Perfect for listening, you know.) Well, the Hendersons have a lovely family, but their marriage is over. They yell all the time, you know. He yells and she yells, and she says she has seen a divorce lawyer and he says to go ahead. And little Tyler hides..."

"Enough!" said Alex. "We don't want to hear about anyone or anything else. You can keep your gossip to yourself. We just want to know who you've been reporting to. Who did you tell about us...about the books?"

"I told you, I don't know. I don't know who he is. Oh, there are so many interesting things to tell. Why do you only keep asking about him?"

"If you don't know his name, just tell us where he is. Where do you go to talk to him?"

"I really don't think he would like that, no I don't. He's a very good listener, just I said. Oh yes, I wasn't lying. I've learned not to lie to you. But he isn't very nice, you know. I don't really think he'd be very happy with little Sarty if he knew I had told. No I'd better not tell. Just think of that creek, though, going all dry. Very sad, I can tell you. A lovely creek, all dry as a bone now. That's what the farmer said, dry as a bone. He's quite upset about it."

"We don't care about the creek!" said Adam. "Just tell us where you talk to this nameless person!"

"Just listen. You aren't listening. No, I don't think you are good listeners, at all. I am telling what I know. I am answering your questions. But there can't be names. He'd know if I told you the name, and then he'd be angry. He was very specific. No talking to humans. No telling them gossip. No giving them information. I don't want to make him angry. Then who would listen to all that I've heard? No, I tell you just this, and I know you are clever. You will know what to do. You won't be angry with Sarten any more. You'll go your way, doing all the fun and interesting things I heard you talking about, and you'll leave little Sarty alone. I'm just listening, after all. I'm not hurting anyone."

"If you've been listening, Sarten, you know that you have been hurting us," said Alex. "When you tell whoever it is about us and our books, he comes and steals them."

"Oh, maybe. But, really, you don't know that that's true. For all you know you've just misplaced them. Or it could have been anyone who broke in and stole them. There have been some amazing break-ins in this town, I can tell you. Just the other week, over on Elm Street..."

169

"We don't care," said Dominic with finality. "You know full well who is breaking in and stealing the books. Tell us where you go to talk to him."

"Well, I really don't like the tone you are all taking. I tell you, I'm only an innocent little muxen. I've done as you asked. I've talked and I've gossiped, even though he said not to. But no information. Oh no. He would be angry. He said absolutely no information to humans. Humans are rabble rousers. Humans are dangerous. They…"

"What?" broke in Adam. "Did you say humans are dangerous?"

"Oh, yes. Yes, yes. He said so, and I'm afraid it's true. Most everyone knows it."

"You're right," said Dominic quietly. "We are dangerous." He applied a bit more pressure. "So now where exactly is this 'he'?"

"I really can't. You don't understand."

More pressure.

"Okay, okay. A…a farm," The little muxen choked on the word and began to cough. "A creek." He gagged. "A field…a cave…" The last word was strangled off in a fit of hacking and heaving.

"What's wrong with him?" cried Eve.

Dominic was looking at the creature in his hand with horrified disgust as it writhed and gagged. With a sudden shake, he dropped it to the ground.

170

Quick as a blink, the little lizard sat up, flashed them a saucy wink and dashed off through the thick grass.

Dominic cursed and Adam laughed, but Logan gave a sharp whistle.

A flash of pink appeared, streaking off across the field, and then it was gone.

"What a little faker," said Eve.

"I can't believe I fell for that," Dominic said.

"We all did," said Alex. "I thought you had killed it there for a minute."

"Well, at least we know how to make sure we aren't being spied on now," Eve said. "That was quick thinking about the whistle, Logan. It must be the noise that makes him turn pink like that."

"Oh," said Alex. "Is that what that was about?"

"Well, we may not know where to find the thief, but we know where to start looking," said Logan. "A farm with a sign over the gate, a dry creek, a field and a cave. That's better than nothing."

"A little better than nothing," grumped Adam. "But there must be a hundred farms around here. What are we going to do? Ride around on our bikes for miles personally looking at every farm?"

"If we have to, I guess we will," said Eve. "But I was thinking that we should start with a map. We could check out where the creeks are."

"But there are probably a hundred creeks, too. And maps aren't going to show the individual farms. They'll just have the roads on them."

"Determined to be positive, aren't we, Adam? I'm just saying it would be a place to start."

"Eve's right," said Alex. "We have to start somewhere."

"Great. Next up on our thrilling adventures…the library."

* * * * *

After a couple of hours of searching through endless maps for something useful, Logan was feeling about as negative as Adam. There were road maps for tourists, surveying maps, even agricultural maps, but none that listed the names of any of the farms. And, as Adam had predicted, there were dozens of creeks running through the farmland. Unfortunately, none of them were marked *dried up creek by field with cave.* Now that would have been a good map. Instead, most of them weren't marked at all. Plus, Dominic pointed out just when they were all really in the mood for more discouragement; there were probably tons of creeks that were too small to make it on the maps.

172

"And you couldn't have made that observation before we wasted half the afternoon in the library?" snapped Eve.

"He probably thought it was obvious," said Adam nastily.

Logan sighed. He had a pain between his shoulder blades from hunching over for so long, and the bickering wasn't helping. He stood up and stretched and looked out the narrow window at the trees that shaded the parking lot. The trees really were the best part of this town. They were everywhere. *Perfect for listening*, he suddenly remembered. That muxen must have a heyday here. Where was it he had said had such great listening trees? Oh, yeah, the Hendersons. Lovely family.

Then it hit him. The Hendersons. Without a word to the others, he turned and headed for the front desk.

"Hey, Logan, are you leaving just like that?" called Adam.

"I just thought of something."

He asked the librarian at the desk for a phone book and flipped to the H's. There were at least ten Hendersons listed, but one caught his eye immediately: Henderson, Richard P. 414 Elm St.

Elm Street. That was it. That had to be it. He threw the phone book down on the table in front of Alex in triumph, pointing to the entry he'd found.

"Henderson, Richard P.?" Alex asked.

"Elm St. The Hendersons live on Elm St." said Logan. "Remember the gossip that Sarten was so keen to share with us? The Hendersons are fighting. There was a break in on Elm St. Maybe those were places near the place he couldn't tell us about."

"You're totally right," said Alex. She grabbed a book of road maps and flipped to the index. "Elm street....Elm street. Here it is. Page 3, section D1." There was a pause while she hunted it down. "Yes! Elm St. It's right at the edge of town. It looks like it ends in open fields. I'll bet you anything those fields are where we'll find our farm. Logan, you're a genius."

Chapter 14

Fear Perched Like a Bird

Eager to get started, Adam arrived twenty minutes early to the Redoubt the next morning. Of course, he was the first one there, so he passed the time by pacing restlessly around the circle.

"Geesh, Adam, 8:00 wasn't early enough for you?" Alex dropped her backpack to the ground and yawned. Still, Adam noticed that she was there five minutes early herself. He tried to relax some, and sat down next to her, leaning against a tree to wait for the others.

At 8:00 on the nose, they could see Dominic heading toward them from across the field. He had one of the photocopies they'd made of the map in his hand and Alex's book under his arm. Alex looked relieved to see it. They had agreed that Dominic should keep it at his house since it was unlikely that Sarten had any chance to discover who he was or where he lived yet.

"Did you guys notice this?" asked Dominic, waving the map at them as he sat down.

"Notice what?"

"This spot right here."

He pointed at the map. Sure enough, right there in the empty fields across from Elm St. there was a shaded patch.

"It's probably just a flaw in the photocopy," said Adam.

"I thought that, too, at first, but look at how even it is. And it's a perfect square. The more I look at it, the more I think that's the farm we're looking for."

Alex was looking impressed, and for some reason this bothered Adam. "Oh, come on. It's just a smudge."

"Just a smudge, like those are just clouds? Like this is just a circle of trees? Like that thing we talked to yesterday was just a chameleon?"

"I think he's right," said Alex. She was looking at her own copy. "It's like the map shows a shadow where the farm would be. I didn't notice anything like that on the original, but I'm sure that's what it is."

Adam was unconvinced, but he knew better than to keep arguing. They'd find out soon enough if Dominic's theory was correct.

They lapsed into silence, waiting for Logan and Eve. As the minutes passed, Adam could feel his impatience growing. Why would they be late today of all days? This could be the day they finally found some answers.

It was fifteen minutes before Logan appeared, and he didn't look happy.

"I went by Eve's house to walk with her, and she can't come," he reported without even greeting them. "I guess she and her mom got in a huge fight, and she's grounded. And her mom is watching her, so I don't think she's going to be able to sneak out. I wasn't allowed in to see her, but Eve dropped this out the window."

He held out a note. Alex took it and read it out loud.

"Guys, I'm so sorry about this. My mom figured out that we were lying about being in a play, and when I couldn't explain what we were really doing, she freaked out. She says I'm grounded for the rest of the summer, but don't worry. She'll let me off after a few days. I'll just have to be more careful from now on. I'm really sorry I can't go check out that farm today. If you want to go without me, I'll totally understand. Just let me know what you find. If you send a text to my sister's phone, I'll be able to get it. I'm borrowing it for a while. Sorry, Eve."

Alex looked up. "What are we going to do?"

"What do you mean, 'what are we going to do?'" said Adam. "We're going to go the farm,

177

find out what's going on, and leave a note for Eve about it."

Logan looked down and kicked at a tuft of grass.

"I don't think that's a good idea," said Dominic.

"Me either," said Alex.

"Why not?" asked Adam. A feeling of frustrated impatience was rising as he sensed what was about to happen. "You don't think we should go without Eve? She told us to go ahead. And this is really important. We need to find this guy before he steals more books. And Eve is supposed to be grounded all summer. We can't wait that long."

"She said she'd probably get off in a few days," said Logan.

"We don't know what we're going to find," Alex said. "It would be better if we were all together."

"But you and I went to see the Gylf by ourselves, and we didn't know anything about them."

"That was before we met the others. And I'd seen one of them before. We don't know *anything* about this guy except that he's bad. I just think it's better…safer…if we all go together."

"We're just going to check it out," said Adam, knowing he was going to lose this argument, but unable to let it go. "Just because the guy's a thief doesn't mean that he is dangerous. And even if he is, what is Eve going to do? It's not like she's a martial arts master or anything."

"I know," said Alex. "But I just have a feeling that we're better off when we're all together."

Adam groaned. Apparently now that they'd established that they had to trust her feelings, she was going to use that excuse to get her way all the time. Why bother to have reasons for things when you've got Alex's feelings?

"Besides," said Logan. "If we do find something important, it's not fair to leave Eve out of it. We're all in this together."

"I agree," Dominic said.

All three looked at Adam. He bit back all the insults of Eve that jumped into his mind, knowing that they wouldn't be convincing and would only make him look like a jerk. He felt free to think them though. He couldn't remember ever feeling so frustrated. This was it; he was sure of it. At this farm, they were going to find the answers. And knowing that, just going home and doing nothing today felt impossible. But there was clearly no convincing the others. He wasn't going to argue if they were determined, but that didn't mean he couldn't have a little look around by himself.

"Fine," he said. "If you all want to wait, we'll wait. I just hope Eve can join us some time this year."

"I'm sure it won't be long," said Logan. "Eve's mom seems like the kind who blows up and then gets over it later."

"So what should we do today?" asked Alex. "Do you guys want to go see the Gylf?"

"If we can't all be together, we should probably not do anything," said Adam.

Dominic ignored him. "I'd like to meet them."

"I'm in," Logan said.

Alex looked at Adam.

"Not today," he said, and then, trying to seem like he was okay, "You guys go ahead. I'm just not in the mood."

"What are you going to do?"

Logan was looking at him strangely, and Adam began to rummage in his backpack to have an excuse to look down, "I'll probably just go home. My mom has been nagging me to mow the lawn anyway. She'll be thrilled I'm home to do it. Do you mind if I borrow your book for today? Maybe when I finish the lawn I'll get a chance to read. Without my own, it's been a while since I got to read it."

Alex nodded and handed it over.

"Okay. Well, I'll text Eve and tell her what we decided," she said. "I'll tell her to call me as soon as she's un-grounded. Hmm...I guess I'd better find my phone if I'm going to do that."

"Sounds good." Adam wasn't really listening. He had the uncomfortable feeling that Logan was still watching him, so he didn't look around as he grabbed his backpack, but just called over his shoulder. "See you guys later."

He continued in the direction of home until he was quite sure they were gone. Then, looking around quickly, he turned and headed toward Elm St.

Stubbornly determined not to follow Dominic's hunch about the dark spot on the map, Adam scouted the farms around Elm street for over an hour, getting hot and tired before he was finally forced admit that Dom must have been right. He'd seen several creeks, and even one that was low enough to be almost dry, but there were no caves that he could find. Now the only farm he hadn't visited was the one marked with the shaded square. That fact did not improve his mood.

The property line of the farm in question was marked with a shoulder-high barbed wire fence. The first field Adam saw was just grass with a few cows grazing far back from the road. Beyond that he could see a field of some kind of grain. The farmhouse was not in sight, but Adam thought it must be further down the road where he could see a small cluster of trees. He wasn't sure whether he felt disappointed or vindictively satisfied that there was no creek in sight.

With no way over the fence, Adam took to the road again and headed toward the trees in the distance. As he approached, he could see the small, neat farmhouse sheltering beneath their branches. A pick-up truck was parked in the

181

gravel drive, but there was no one in sight. Once he had passed the trees, he could make out a dark green line on the other side of another grassy field. It had to be a creek of some kind. Adam turned off the road.

Closer up, the bushes growing along the creek bed looked dry and brittle. He quickened his pace through the tall grass. Pushing his way through the bushes, Adam found himself on the top of a fairly steep drop off to the all but dry creek bed below. It was only about six feet down, so he grabbed hold of some roots and slid down.

It was hard to see very far in either direction, as the creek did not run straight, but he decided to head away from the farmhouse, walking slowly along the dry bed and looking carefully for any signs of a cave.

Adam had braced himself for a long search, but as it turned out, it was right around the first bend in the creek. On the far embankment, mostly covered with drying vines but still plainly visible, was a hole, big enough that he could have walked through it without even having to hunch over.

Adam stopped dead in his tracks. This was it. He had no doubt about it. But what should he do now? His intention had been to find the cave and then go tell the others. But now that he was here, it seemed like such a waste to just turn around and walk away. For several minutes, he stood there staring at the cave mouth. Then his good sense took over and he turned away.

Once through the trees on the top of the embankment, he looked around for something to mark the spot, so he could easily find it when they all came back together. But before he found anything suitable, he saw a little house, a shack actually, only about fifty feet from where he was standing. It was covered by thickly growing trees all around and there were no lights on, but Adam was positive that someone was standing in the doorway looking at him.

He froze, thinking of trespassing charges and vicious dogs.

After a few minutes of nothing happening, he began to think he had just imagined the shadowy figure. Telling himself he was being paranoid, he turned and spotted a big stone, perfect for marking the location. He picked it up and carried it over to the gap in the bushes that he had just come through. In front of the stone, he laid a long stick pointing from the road to the creek and the cave. It was the best he could do.

He was still kneeling next to the stick when a voice made him jump.

"It looks suspiciously like you are marking something."

Adam leapt to his feet and left his stomach behind on the ground.

"Thought we were being oh-so-secret, did we?"

Turning this way and that in startled confusion, Adam couldn't see anyone. Then a very nasty chuckle from the direction of the wooden shack clued him in. Now he could see the figure in the doorway quite clearly, a short, masculine figure with long straggly hair. The man's attempt at laughter was more like gravel in

183

a blender than like anything resembling humor. Adam's initial panic settled into real fear.

"That look on your face is about the most entertaining thing I've seen in years. It's almost a pity that you're leaving now and never coming back."

A pointed silence followed this statement, and Adam quickly turned to go.

"Now that I think of it," the voice stopped him, "you can move that little marker, too. You won't be needing to remember this place. Whatever you've got floating around in your adolescent brain, you can forget it. Throw that junk off into the trees before you go. Come on now. Hop to it."

Adam hesitated but didn't see any help for it. He returned to his marker and threw the stick back in to the woods. The rock proved more tricky. It was too heavy to throw, so he settled for rolling it back to its original location. In the end, it wouldn't really matter, he thought as he worked. He wasn't going to forget this place. They'd just have to climb down to the creek at another spot and then follow it along to the cave.

Everything would have been fine if his backpack hadn't slipped off his shoulder. With a grunt of frustration, he dragged it along with rock and then yanked it back up on his shoulder as he turned to go. Unfortunately, one of the straps was caught under the rock, and the backpack tore open as he turned spilling all the contents onto the ground. Adam cursed under his breath.

The cackle from the shack was cut short as Adam hurriedly gathered up his stuff. He scarcely had time to hear the heavy breathing of the man coming toward him before a thin hand with filthy nails snatched the Book of Sight from his hands.

"Gods of stone!   You have the book." There was a long pause, while Adam stared at the bearded man and the man stared at the book. Then without warning, the man turned and hobbled back into his house, taking the book with him.

Adam sprinted after him without even thinking but was forced to pause when he reached the doorway, waiting for his eyes to adjust to a gloom deeper than any he had ever experienced before. He was still straining to see some movement in the black room before him when a spark suddenly illuminated a pair of trembling hands.

The man was standing over a table, holding the large red book away from his body. It was on fire.

With a cry, Adam launched himself at the man. There was a brief scuffle, in which Adam got a little singed, but the dirty stranger was clearly not in a condition to put up much of a fight. A few minutes later, Adam was backing towards the door, beating the smoking book against his leg to put out the last of the fire.

"You don't know what you're doing, kid." The man slumped breathlessly into a rickety chair, his face turned away. "You'd be better off rid of that gods-cursed thing."

Adam stopped short. "You...you've read it?"

"Have I read it?" The man gave a demented laugh. "Oh, I've read it, curse the day I ever laid eyes on it."

"But the Book of Sight..."

"Sight? Sight?! You don't want that kind of sight, kid. Take my word for it. Oh I see you, eyes shining, oh-so-eager. I know what you're thinking. It's so special, so wonderful, like being a privileged member of a secret club. I am different. I know things others don't. I can see. *See.*" He spat the word. "But you haven't seen it all yet, kid. Not even close. Wait long enough and you'll start seeing the other things. The dark things. The ugly things. The things you'll wish you could forget. And then you'll realize that they can see you, too."

Adam stood transfixed.

"Scared? You have no idea what you've gotten into. You should let me finish off that book before it's too late."

This brought Adam to life. "Are...are you the one who stole our other books?"

"*Our other books?* There are others? There are others..." A spasm passed over the man's body. Then he suddenly burst out, "Fools! Get out! *Get out!*"

But Adam was unable to walk away from so many possible answers. "How did you..."

186

"GET OUT!" The man practically jumped across the table, lunging at Adam, and for the first time Adam saw his face. The word deformed did not begin to describe it. A criss-cross of raised scars obliterated any expression and the hair on his forehead was entirely burned off. One eye had been brutally slashed and stared white and blind in the darkness.

Adam turned and ran.

Chapter 15

Subterranean Levels of Courage

Every time he was with the Gylf, Logan felt like he was in a dream. He had thought after that first time that he would eventually get used to it, that it would all start feeling more normal, but it didn't. So far, the feeling that he had crossed over into another world when he entered their forest was stronger each time.

This time was particularly strange since they were introducing Dominic to the Gylf for the first time. Logan hated showing other people things that were important to him. He tried to soothe the twisting in his stomach by reminding himself that Dominic had shown them the village, that if he loved that place he would love this one, too. It didn't help much. A sidelong glance at Alex told him she was nervous, too.

Dominic was better than most at hiding his feelings. All through his first sight of the Gylf home and the introductions to Celana and Terra and the others he was polite, but his face was impassive. Adam was partially right, though when he called Logan 'the mind reader.' Dominic may have been expressionless, but Logan could see the fire that burned deep in his eyes. Logan relaxed. Dominic got it.

The whole day was close to perfect. After welcoming Dominic with a rousing welcoming dance, the Gylf scattered to their respective tasks. A young Gylf named Flax, red-haired and wearing clothes the exact shade of a blade of grass, was their guide for the day, spending several hours walking through the forest, teaching them the names of the different kinds of vines and how to identify the seven patterns of vine weaving. They were joined for lunch next to the stream by several other Gylf who were in the area. A few of these were gray-haired, though very young, and took them after to a flat rocky area to teach them a game called stone tumbling.

As far as Logan could tell, it was a cross between bowling and pool. You made a stack of eight stones and then used another one to knock them down, trying to make them land on certain marks that had been carved into the rocky ground. Logan was just taking his first turn, a round flat stone fitted perfectly in his palm, when Adam burst into the clearing, looking wild. Logan dropped the rock with a dull thud.

"What happened to the book?"

Adam's eyes widened at the question, and he backed away a step. There was a moment's silence. Then wordlessly Adam turned and took

190

Alex's book out of his bag amid a small cloud of dust. The once red cover was mostly black.

Alex cried out and snatched it from his hands, opening it frantically. The edges of each page were totally burned, and soot had obliterated nearly all that was left. She sank to the ground, staring at it in horror. The Gylf crowded comfortingly around her.

"What happened?" asked Logan as calmly as he could.

Adam began to recount his whole adventure in faltering words. He was clearly ashamed to admit that he had lied to them and searched for the cave on his own, but no one was concerned with much other than what had happened to the book. When Adam had told it all, he knelt down next to Alex.

"I'm so sorry, Alex. I should never have been there. I should never have borrowed your book and I shouldn't have lied to you. I'm so sorry this happened."

Alex had tears on her face, but she nodded.

"So is this one-eyed man our thief, then?" asked Dominic, carefully avoiding looking at Alex.

"I don't think so," said Adam.

"You don't think so?" said Alex. "He burned my book!"

"I know, but you didn't see him. He was so shocked to see it at first. And when I mentioned others, he just... Well, there's no way he had any idea."

"But he could have been lying, pretending. He's obviously capable of..." She held up the book.

"Yeah, but I don't think anyone could pretend that well." Alex started to reply, but Adam cut her off. "And even if they could, this guy could not have stolen the books the way they were stolen. He was... I'm telling you, you didn't see him. It's not just his eye. There's no way this guy has been more than ten feet from his little shack in years."

Alex was silent.

"So that brings us back to the cave," said Dominic.

"It's the one," said Adam. "I know it. I don't know who or what is in there, but I know it's the one."

"I still think we need to worry about this one-eyed man before we worry about the cave," said Alex. "We wanted to find someone else who had read the book, and now we have. We can't just skip over that."

"If you'd been there, you wouldn't be so anxious to go back," muttered Adam.

"What?"

"Look," Adam burst out. "I've been thinking about it all the way over here. This book is amazing and I wouldn't want to have missed the stories or the things I've seen for the world. But what if this guy is right? What if seeing these things is a lot more dangerous than we know? What if there's no way to realize how bad it is until it's too late? I don't know what I think about it all, and I can't believe I'm going to say this, but someone has to. There's no doubt in my mind that there's something in that cave, only we don't have a clue what it is. It could be deadly, for all we know. Do we really want to risk our lives to recover a book that we know next to nothing about?"

Logan could feel the silence in the pit of his stomach.

Alex set her destroyed book on the grass as carefully as if it were made of glass.

"Yes," she said.

No one responded.

"Why don't we ask the Gylf?" said Logan turning to the three who stood grouped around Alex's knee. "Do you know anything about this cave or this thief?"

"We do not," answered the one called Pedlan, "but it may be that the grandfathers know something that we are unaware of."

There was nothing to be done, then, but troop back toward the Gylf home in search of the grandfathers. Logan led the gloomy, silent group, trying hard not to think too much about anything but the hope that the Gylf might have something helpful to say.

Unfortunately, they did not. Four of the grandparents were at home, and they listened with genuine concern, but shook their heads.

"I am sorry, but we know very little of humans and their affairs," said Terfol. "And this cave is unknown to us. Our knowledge of the world is limited to our forest home."

"Have you never seen anyone or anything in the forest that could be this thief?" asked Dominic.

"Didn't the men the Dund saw use the word 'pilpi' to describe him?" added Alex.

A look of recognition came over the Gylf faces. "There is a creature called Pilpi spoken of in one of our traditions. It is known as a creature of darkness, a shadow seeker," said Celana.

"It is only mentioned very briefly," said Flew, one of the younger grandfathers. "We have never seen such a creature in my lifetime."

"Nor mine," said Terfol, "but we had never seen a human with sight, either. This shadow seeker may indeed be a thief of light."

"I'm afraid that doesn't help you know more about what you might find if you encounter him," said Celana.

"No, but thank you for telling us what you know," Alex said. "If you are right, now at least we know it isn't human, whatever it is."

"Will you go to this cave?" asked Flew.

"I think we have to," Alex replied.

"Would some of you come with us?" Adam asked. Logan felt his heart leap at the idea and then crash down again at Terfol's reply.

194

"I am sorry, but that is not possible. It is not for us to leave our forest home. Our work is here."

"You mean none of you have ever left here?"

"Why should we? This place is ours to enjoy and the forest needs us as we need it. There is enough here to occupy us for all of our long lives."

"But don't you wonder what else is out there?" asked Alex.

Celana smiled. "Our all is here. The Gylf were created for this place, for this purpose. We have no need for anything else. We are content."

"But if there are evil creatures out there, you could help other people be safe from them," said Adam.

"That is not the role of the Gylf," said Flew. "We exist to care for our home and rejoice in it. That is why we were made."

Logan admired their peaceful confidence, but he felt somehow let down. Didn't they care about anyone but themselves?

"It is difficult for you to understand," said Terfol. "You are human. Humans have a different purpose. To you has been given the job of rousing and defending."

"How do you know that?" asked Adam. "I thought you didn't know much about humans."

"We do not," said Celana, "but the traditions say one thing of you. Humans are the rabble-rousers, the dangerous ones, a threat to the world and its best defense." She smiled at the look on their faces. "This is not the first you have heard of this, I see."

"So why weren't you afraid of us?" asked Dominic.

"What is there to fear? If a dangerous role has been given to you, it must be for a purpose. When each one fulfills his purpose, the world is as it should be."

"Besides," added Flew, "all that is dangerous is not evil. Is not a deer a threat to the life of a delicate flower? Yet what creature is more graceful and lovely than a deer? In its own way, each creature of the forest is dangerous, but also necessary to all the others."

"So if we're supposed to be the dangerous ones, I guess that means we don't have much choice about the cave," said Adam.

"There is always a choice," said Terfol. "Only let peace and not fear guide your steps. Nothing will bring you greater joy than walking the path for which you were made."

Chapter 16

A Dark Hungry Mouth

"**I** still think we need to go back to see the one-eyed man. He knows things, and maybe he'd be more likely to tell us if we were all there together."

"I've already told you, Alex, he's completely twisted. I wouldn't trust anything that came out of his mouth." Adam's voice was sharp. "It's a dead end. Our only choices are to explore this cave and try to find the pilpi thing or to give it up and be happy sharing the one book we've got left." He sighed. "Anyway, there isn't any point in arguing about it right now. We can't decide anything until Eve is here, too."

After two days of nothing but hanging out at the Redoubt, going over and over everything they knew, Dominic was sick of the whole thing.

He agreed that they needed to wait for Eve to make any decisions, but he would rather spend this time doing something useful instead of standing around repeating the same questions and theories. He had still never been to the field where the strange creature called Dund lived, and he'd only had that one day with the Gylf.

He was about to suggest a visit to the Dund when Logan cut across whatever Alex was saying. "Eve!"

They all jumped up. Eve was making her way across the field toward them.

Dominic never would have thought he'd be so glad to see her. Everyone was talking at once, welcoming Eve back, filling her in, asking her how she got her mom to let her go.

At that, Eve looked very unhappy. "I didn't, really."

"You mean you snuck out?" said Adam.

"Not exactly. My mom is gone for two days to a scrapbooking seminar or something. After she left, I just asked my dad if I could go out, and he said yes."

Dominic was thinking about everything he'd ever heard about girls being trouble. This one certainly was. Apparently some guys thought that was interesting or attractive. He just thought it was a little psycho. It was also, fortunately, not his problem.

"Won't she be mad when she comes back?" asked Alex.

Eve snorted. "Maybe. But if she's upset, I'll tell her I had Dad's permission. Then she'll be mad at him instead of me. Anyway I had to come," she rushed on. "My book is gone."

Their horrified faces made her look even more miserable. "I'm so sorry, you guys. It's all my fault. I was going crazy locked up in the house like that and the book was the only thing that was keeping me sane. I got a little careless about hiding it, and last night my mom found it on one of her raids of my room. She went ballistic, started yelling and carrying on. I know I should have stayed calm and tried to talk her down, but I just snapped. I said a bunch of stupid things that made her even madder and then she carried the book to the outside trash can and smashed it in there with some really foul stuff. I waited until everyone was asleep last night and then quietly went out to get it, but it was gone. Totally gone. I promise you, I even looked through all the coffee grounds and banana peels. The thief must have gotten it. It's awful. I didn't sleep at all last night. I'm so sorry. It's just a good thing we still have your book, Alex."

Alex made a choking sound, and Adam filled Eve in as succinctly as possible. When he was done, Eve's face was resolute.

"We need to get those books back," she said, "and we need to do it today. I know we didn't ask for any of this to happen, but it did. We've read what we've read and we've seen what we've seen. I don't know about anyone else, but I can't just pretend that never happened and I won't go back to life as it used to be. Apparently none of the other creatures we've met so far are able to do anything about this thief, so it's up to us. Like they said, humans are the dangerous ones, right?"

"So do we go to the one-eyed man or to the cave?" asked Adam.

"Both," said Eve without hesitating, and surprisingly, no one argued.

They settled the details so quickly that Dominic knew he wasn't the only one who was relieved the waiting was over.

* * * * *

Dominic arrived first at the designated meeting spot, not because he had particularly hurried, but because he'd already packed his gear the night before. He hadn't known for sure when he'd be needing it, but it just made sense to have it all ready. There wasn't much to it anyway, just a flashlight, some granola bars, a bottle of water, and a sweatshirt in case it was cold inside the cave.

To pass the time, Dominic stretched out on the grass and looked up at the clouds. He'd never paid much attention to cloud pictures before, but the others claimed that once you had read the book, the cloud pictures could actually tell you things. There wasn't much to see, only three or four little puffs.

As he lay and looked, though, he did begin to think that the smallest one looked exactly like the face of a girl with her head turned partially away. He could trace out one eye and a slight smile and those wisps on the side would be her hair. Still not much different that when he had played cloud pictures with his mother as a child.

His mother. Now that he thought of it, something about the face of the girl-cloud drifting innocently along reminded him of her. A stupid thought probably, but it made him smile anyway. Then a shadow passed over his face, and he realized that a larger cloud was drifting toward the girl-cloud. This new cloud had no particular form, but the front did open up in what looked alarmingly like a mouth full of vicious teeth.

Irrationally, he felt afraid for the girl-cloud. If they continued on their present course, the two clouds would soon collide. It seemed awful to think of that gaping mouth swallowing her peaceful face.

He tried to tell himself that he was being ridiculous. Clouds are just a bunch of water vapor and dust particles. But was it just his imagination that the girl-cloud now had a very frightened look on her face? They were very close now, and a long arm-like tendril was snaking out from the monster-cloud toward the girl-cloud. It connected with her hair and her mouth opened. Dominic was sure she was screaming. Two eyes were now very clear in the monster-cloud face, and its mouth opened even wider.

Dominic whispered, "No!"

Then he noticed a third cloud, long and thin like a knife moving toward the monster-cloud. With a swiftness that had nothing to do with wind speeds, it plunged into the monster-cloud's right eye. The tendril arm released the girl-cloud's hair. The monster dropped back, and the next thing Dominic knew, the monster-cloud and the girl-cloud were drifting apart again. The knife was gone.

"Are you okay?"

Dominic's head snapped up. Eve was standing over him, looking concerned.

"Were you cloud-watching? You look like you just saw a ghost."

"Yeah. Well, not a ghost. But it was weird."

He wasn't sure if he wanted to tell her about it, but she just stood there, looking at him expectantly, so he did. When he was done, her eyes were wide. Dominic felt torn between relief that she clearly believed it was real and annoyance that she was going to make a big deal out of it. He could see Alex and Logan coming from one direction and Adam from the other, so he hastily changed the subject.

"I guess this is really going to be it then. Everyone looks all ready to go."

"Yeah," Eve was quiet for a minute. "But what makes them?"

"What makes what?"

"The cloud pictures. Clouds are just a natural formation. How could they possibly be making pictures that we were meant to read? Who or what could possibly do that?"

"I have no idea."

"Sometimes I think maybe we're all just going crazy."

"All at the same time?"

"Would it be any weirder than the clouds sending us messages?"

Dominic smiled. "No, I guess not."

Eve took a deep breath and seemed to shake off her dark mood. "Well," she said, "If I had to go crazy, I'm glad I got to do it with other people. It's a lot more fun than going crazy alone. Should we go meet them?"

Following Adam toward the shack and the cave, Dominic noticed that Adam had brought the short sword that he found in the Gylf woods. It was tucked under his belt and hanging down by his side. The seriousness of what they were doing hit Dominic at once.

"Can we just stop for a minute?" he asked.

The others did, looking at him strangely. For a second he felt really awkward, but he knew this was too important to skip. "I've just realized that we never talked about what we're going to do if we actually find this thief. I mean, maybe we'll just be exploring and find no one. Or maybe we'll get lucky and find a stash of stuff and get our books back with no problem. But what if we do find the thief? What exactly is our plan?"

"We'll get our books back," said Alex

"Right, and after going to so much trouble to steal them, he's just going to let us take them?"

"No, probably not, but we have to try."

"I don't think we can really have a plan," said Adam. "We don't even know if we're going to find anything, or what it will be if we do. How can we possibly know how to handle it?"

"True," Logan said. "I think what Dominic means is what are we *willing* to do? I mean, you have that sword, and I'm not saying it's a bad idea to have it. But I don't know if I'm ready to go in there to attack someone, even to get the books back."

"Yeah," said Dominic. "I just think we should all say what we're thinking."

"But did you ever think that whoever...or whatever...this is might attack *us*? That's why I brought the sword. For protection. In case we have to defend ourselves."

"I think that was a really good idea," said Eve.

"Me too," Alex added. "But I do think it should be for defense only. We're not going to attack. We're going to try to get back what is ours. We don't need to hurt anyone unless they are hurting us."

"I agree," said Dominic.

Logan nodded.

"Okay then," Adam said a little impatiently. "Now that we have that settled, let's get on with it."

In the end, they could have saved themselves all the debate about whether or not to visit the one-eyed man's shack because when they got there, it was empty. The door was wide open and all the furniture was still there, but there was no sign of the man. All the cupboards were empty, as was the closet. A thick layer of dust was over everything (although Adam thought that might have been the case even when the man lived there). If it hadn't been for Alex's charred book and a matching burn spot on the wooden table, Dominic might have thought Adam made the whole thing up. It was disappointing not to find the man, but at least it made the decision of what to do next a whole lot easier. Lingering in the mold-infested shack was not appealing to anyone.

Ten minutes later, they were standing in front of the overgrown opening to the cave. For just a moment, everyone looked at each other, feeling the same nervous excitement. This was it. They were here.

Then Dominic stepped forward and started pulling the vines away from the mouth of the cave. Logan and Adam hurried to help him. It didn't take long to clear the way. In a matter of minutes, a gaping dark opening stood awaiting them.

They all took out their flashlights. There was another pause, and it was Dominic again who squared his shoulders and walked in. He was picturing in his mind the face of that young man in his mother's painting, unafraid and determined. He hoped he looked that brave right now, even if he didn't feel it.

The cave was dry and gravelly inside, and the others crowding behind him soon cut off what little light he had. Creeping forward, he flipped on his flashlight, but before he could raise it, a searing pain cut across his face. Instinctively, he threw up a hand, only to experience the same burning across his forearm. The shock and pain were so severe that he dropped to his knees in the gravelly dirt of the cave floor.

His yell of pain stopped the others instantly. There was a general scuffle and the sound of everyone talking at once, then a light was shining in his face and Alex was standing over him.

"Are you all right?" Her questioning look collapsed into lines of worry. "Oh my gosh...are you okay?...guys come here."

"What happened?" asked Adam. He, too, shined his light in Dominic's face. "Oh man. Okay, no one go any further. Let's get him out of the cave into the light."

Dominic's face and arm were still throbbing and burning, but it was the reactions of the others that really scared him. "What's wrong?"

"You're bleeding," said Alex.

"It's going to be okay," said Adam.

Once out in the light, Dominic put his good hand up to his face. He could feel blood

207

dripping down from two horizontal slashes across his cheek and nose. His right arm had similar cuts, but these crisscrossed a little bit. Both arm and face were stinging like crazy, but the cuts didn't look too deep.

"What the..." said Eve. "What happened?"

Alex had pulled a first aid kit from her backpack and began applying gauze pads to the cuts.

"I don't know. I was just walking along and then I felt this pain on my face. I threw up my arm, and whatever got my face cut my arm, too."

"It doesn't look too deep," said Alex, "but it won't stop bleeding. We need to get you to the clinic. You might need stitches."

"No, we're not leaving yet. It's just some cuts. If you disinfect them, they'll be fine until we're done in the cave."

"But the blood is soaking through the bandages. I only brought a little travel first aid kit from the car. What if you keep bleeding?"

"It's not..."

"Wait," broke in Eve. "I have an idea. The Gylf showed me this plant the other day when we were there. Terra said they use it for wounds. To stop bleeding. I don't know if I can find any around here, but we could try. It had dark green leaves and these little red berries."

Logan sucked in his breath. "You mean like this?" He carefully took out a small wreath of branches covered with red berries.

"Yes!" Eve was elated. "Where did you get that?"

"Terra was wearing it that first day we visited them. She gave it to me when we left."

"That's amazing. It's like someone planned it. Okay, I think we need the juice from the berries to put on the cuts."

Dominic sat and tried not to watch his blood soaking through the bandages on his arm while the others scuffled around looking for rocks to crush the berries. He closed his eyes but that was almost worse. With his eyes shut he couldn't stop imagining what horrible thing might have caused those cuts.

It was a relief when Eve came back. Her voice sounded nervous. "I'm just going to dab this stuff on with the last gauze pad. Hopefully it won't hurt."

It did hurt.

It also worked. The berries had formed a kind of pink paste which looked disgusting on his arm, but he wasn't bleeding anymore. They had no more bandages to cover his wounds, but it didn't seem like he was going to need them.

Dominic flexed his hand. The burning feeling was gone, replaced by a dull throb. "Okay, we're good to go," he said as confidently as he could.

Logan, as usual, wasn't fooled. "Why don't you take some aspirin for the pain, at least?"

Dominic nodded, and Alex handed over the pills.

"So now we have to figure out what happened," said Adam. "Did you hear anything moving, like something was attacking you?"

"No, there was nothing. It was more like I just walked into something."

"It must be some sort of trap then," Adam said. "A couple of us should go in with our lights on and move really slowly, looking for whatever it was." He stopped for a second and looked right at Alex seriously. "Unless you think that's a bad idea."

She shook her head. "No, it's the only thing to do. It's either that or give up. Dom didn't really have his light the last time. With light we'll hopefully be able to see whatever it is."

Adam nodded, shouldered his pack, turned on his flashlight, and headed into the cave without further conversation.

Logan stood up and went with him.

"Okay," said Eve. "I say we let Adam and Logan be the ones who look for the scary booby trap."

But Dominic had no intention of just sitting outside waiting for something to happen. He got up and moved into the entrance of the cave. He could see the flashlights about 20 feet ahead.

"You should be getting to about where I was," he called out softly. "Do you see anything?"

"Not yet," said Adam. "Oh wait. Yeah. Yeah, there's something here. It's like spider webs or something. It's practically invisible. You can only see it when the light reflects off it. It's covering the entire passage. There's a little gap at the bottom, but I doubt we could squeeze under it."

Dominic looked down at the criss-crossed slashes on his arm. Spider-webs. That would explain the pattern, but no spider he'd ever heard of made a web strong and sharp enough to cut a person.

"Don't touch it," he said unnecessarily. "I'll get a stick and we'll see if we can knock them down to get through."

He turned to go out, but Eve and Alex were right behind him. They were both carrying long sticks.

Unfortunately, the sticks were not enough. Squeezed together in front of the webs, they each took a turn trying to break through but to no avail. The strands looked thin and delicate like a spider web, but they felt as strong as steel cables. They would give a little under pressure, but only bounce back unbroken. Adam even tried scraping the wall where they connected, but however they were attached, it was too strong for the stick, which crumbled away on the end.

Eve was the last to try. "What are these stupid things?" she panted after a couple of minutes. "It's like we need cable cutters or something. I don't suppose any of you thought to bring along a pair?"

"No," said Dominic, "but Adam did bring a sword."

"Of course!" Alex said. "The sword!"

Adam looked a little doubtful, but he drew the sword out of his belt and held it up carefully to one strand of the web. With only the slightest touch from the sword, the web swung free. A general cheer went up. Grinning, Adam made a few broad swipes, and soon the whole web was hanging limply against the walls. They were through, and no one had any more doubts that they were in the right place.

Chapter 17

Swallowed Up
in the Cold

Eve followed along behind Alex, listening to the thumping of her heart. She had never been crazy about small spaces. Fortunately, this cave was tall enough to stand up in, even if it was now only wide enough to walk single file. She didn't know if she could have faced having to crawl through the dark, with only a weak flashlight to show where she was going. It made her feel panicky just thinking about it.

The ground underneath had been dirt and then gravel and had now changed to rock. They were steadily descending. She wondered how deep underground this cave led. In her imagination, she saw a series of caves twisting and turning, a giant hollow underworld beneath the sleepy little town of Dunmore. The thought gave her a shiver. Then she laughed. Why not? Unexplored caves would be the least of the things that the good people of Dunmore knew nothing about.

"What's so funny?" asked Logan from behind her.

"Nothing."

"Do you hear that noise?"

"What noise?"

"That rushing sound."

Eve listened. She hadn't even noticed, but Logan was right. There was a rustling sound coming from up ahead, just barely heard over the sound of their footsteps.

"Yeah, I hear it."

"It's been slowly getting louder for the last half hour."

"Water," said Dominic's voice from the end of the line. "Look at the walls."

Eve had been keeping her flashlight trained on the floor in front of her, but when she lifted it a little she could see water trickling down the walls on either side. Not much yet, but judging from that sound ahead, there was going to be a lot more. She felt her heart rate speed up a notch.

The rushing sound kept getting louder and louder until she heard Adam call out from the front of the line, and they all stepped unexpectedly into a giant cavern. The weak light from their flashlights was not enough to discover the far walls or the ceiling. Though they couldn't see it, from the sound and the cool dampness of the air they could tell that the water was right ahead of them.

Without saying anything, they moved forward side by side and so close that their arms were touching. Eve thought she would have even liked to be holding hands, but she didn't want to seem like a coward. It felt creepy to cross the big open space in the dark, not knowing what was above her or on either side. An uncomfortable tingle was running down her spine with every step. After a minute, she even began to miss the stifling confines of the narrow passage. It seemed like an eternity, but it wasn't really that long before they were brought up short by a swift river at their feet.

"I guess we found the water," Eve said.

"Can you see the other side?" asked Adam, shining his light as far out as possible.

"No," Alex said, straining forward with her light, too. "These stupid flashlights are too dim to see anything."

"How are we going to get across?" asked Dominic.

"Maybe we don't have to," Adam said. "Maybe what we need is on this side. We haven't explored the rest of this cavern."

Eve seized on that idea. As much as she hated the thought of wandering around in this enormous room, she liked the look of that dark river even less. "Yeah, let's check it out at least before we get all wet."

"We can try," said Alex doubtfully, "but I'm pretty sure we're going to end up having to find a way over."

"One thing at a time," said Adam.

They divided up into two groups, agreeing to follow the river along in each direction until they hit a wall or found something worth reporting. They would meet back in the middle in a half hour at the latest.

It didn't take that long. Eve, Logan, and Dominic came to a wall on their side of the river after only a few minutes of walking. The river seemed to gush straight out of a solid rock face. The opening must have been just enough for the water to go through. It certainly wasn't enough for a person to enter. They followed the rock wall back around until they found the opening to the passage that had brought them here.

It took Adam and Alex longer to meet them back at the river, but their findings had been pretty much the same. The river continued on for quite a ways but then crashed into the rock wall. Alex said that they could barely see the outlet at all through all the spray and churning water. Eve did not find that mental picture reassuring considering that they now had to find a way across.

"As far as I can see," Adam started, "the only way over is to just wade in and try it. It may not be that deep. Maybe we can just walk across."

"That's pretty risky," said Dominic. "We really need some sort of rope or something, so we can hold onto whoever goes out. The water looks like it's moving pretty fast."

"Did anyone bring rope?" asked Eve.

Their silence was the answer.

"Do we need to go back for some?" asked Logan.

"I think we should," said Dominic.

"If we do that, we won't be able to come back until tomorrow. And by then Eve's mom may have found out what happened and grounded her again," protested Adam. "Just let me at least try it first. I'll go slow and turn back if it feels like it's getting too strong."

"I seriously don't think that's a good idea," Dominic said.

Adam turned to Alex. "What do you think?"

Alex stared at the water for a long minute. "I really don't know."

"Okay, then. In the absence of any scary premonitions, I think I'll risk it," said Adam. "And don't worry. I'll be really careful. I promise that I'll come back if it's too deep and we can head home for some rope."

He took off his shoes and socks and left them, along with his backpack and sweatshirt, next to Alex. Slowly he waded into the fast-moving water, gritting his teeth at the cold.

"Is it freezing?" called Eve.

"Only at first. It's actually not that bad once you get used to it." Adam waded out further, slowly disappearing into the darkness.

Eve could just barely make him out when he stopped. The water was above his knees but hadn't reached his waist yet. "I can see the other side," he called back. "I think I'm over half way there. This has got to be as deep as it gets. There's a little pull, but it's not too bad. I think we can make it."

Eve let out a breath she hadn't realized she'd been holding. She could see Adam waiting for their response. "Okay," she said to the others on the bank. "If we're going to get wet, let's get it over with."

"I guess," said Dominic hesitantly. Eve thought he didn't like being proven wrong. "Okay, but let's just go one at a time and move slowly."

"I'll go first," said Eve. "The less time I have to think about it, the better."

"We're coming," Alex shouted to Adam.

Eve stripped off her shoes and socks. "Should I take Adam his stuff with mine?"

"No," Logan said. "The tallest people should carry the stuff. Less chance of it getting wet. Dominic and I can divide it up. No one has anything very heavy."

Not in the mood to argue, Eve stuffed everything into her backpack. Taking a breath to brace herself, she stepped into the water. Adam was right, it *was* cold, but not the bitterly freezing water she was expecting. Encouraged by this hopeful sign, she hurried forward. Adam, still standing in the same spot, called back encouragement to her. As the water rose up to her knees, she began to feel the pull of the current and slowed her steps, being sure to plant her feet carefully. She could see the far bank now and her confidence grew.

"Go ahead," she told Adam. "I'm right behind you."

He nodded and turned.

When she looked up two steps later, he was gone.

"Adam? Adam!"

Eve could hear yelling from the bank behind her, too. Unthinking, she pushed forward, calling Adam's name. It came as such a shock, she didn't even have time to hold her breath. One minute her feet were on solid rock, the next minute they were standing on nothing, and her body was pulled under in a surge of rushing water.

Chapter 18

A Brother's Hand

The second he saw Adam get sucked under the water, a strange sort of purposeful calm came over Dominic. Alex gave a scream and Dominic saw Eve look up. In some horrible way, he knew what was going to happen.

"Eve, stop right there!" he shouted. "Turn back!"

Unhearing, she plunged forward and was swept off her feet in seconds.

Without even realizing he had done it, Dominic had removed his socks and shoes. He could see out of the corner of his eye that Logan had done the same. They both waded into the water.

"Stay right there," he said to Alex. "See if you can find anything that might work as rope."

He didn't turn around to see if she had listened. Logan was a step ahead of him and had almost arrived at the spot where Adam had disappeared. Somehow Dominic knew just what to do.

"Logan, stop. Don't let it pull you. You have to jump in and swim with the current." He saw Logan give a small nod, and together they plunged in.

Cold, vicious water swirled around him, pulling him under. He tried to swim evenly, keeping pace with the current, but he kept crashing his hands and legs into rocks and being knocked off balance. His flashlight was quickly ripped from his hand, and the world was black. If his eyes were going to be useless, he knew he would have to rely on his ears to find the others. But all he could hear was the rushing and gurgling of the water around him. He wondered where Logan was and if he was all right.

He heard a yell and almost simultaneously smashed into a rock wall. For a second the breath was knocked from him, and he knew that he was going to drown. But then an arm bumped his. Instinctively, he took hold and kicked up for air. The frothing water was pinning him to the wall, but he was able to suck in one breath before the current pulled him back down. The next time he struggled to the surface, he felt something jagged hit his head. Without thinking, he reached up and grabbed on, just barely managing to avoid being sucked back under as he gripped a tiny ledge sticking out of the rock face. It was impossible to see anything in the dark, but he thought the arm he was holding was Adam's. It was still flailing in desperation, so Dominic took that as a good sign. At least Adam was still alive. Dominic tightened his grip on the rock ledge.

"Hold still!" he shouted over the roaring of the water. "I have you and I've found something to hold onto."

The flailing stopped. Dominic gave a great heave, fearing the worst, but the next minute Adam was shouting right in his ear.

"Dominic?"

"Yes!" he yelled back. "I can't hold on much longer. Try to grab for the ledge."

He felt Adam's free hand scrabbling on the hard rock and then a sudden relief as the weight of the arm dragging him down was lifted.

"You have a hold?"

"For now."

"We have to move toward the bank. Can you?"

"Yeah."

"I'm letting go of your arm. We both need two hands."

"Okay."

With two hands, Dominic found it possible to slowly creep along the ledge, the water pulling terrifyingly at his body the whole time. His arms were screaming in agony, but he knew if he let go now he'd never get a grip again. After a few minutes that seemed like an eternity, he felt the pull of the water let up slightly. He tried to shout back encouragement to Adam, but wasn't sure if Adam could hear him. Dominic didn't have the energy to check on him. They had to get out of this current now.

A minute later, his right leg bumped into solid rock. At first a terrible fear gripped him. He was boxed in! But then he realized that his arm wasn't touching anything. He slowly let go with his right arm and reached out. It was the bank! With a final heave and a grunt, he pulled himself up on the solid rock and laid his head back, exhausted. Even the relief he felt when Adam clambered up beside him only reached his brain through a haze.

"What about Eve?" asked Adam, panting. "Is she okay?"

Another surge of adrenaline made Dominic sit up. "I don't know. Logan jumped in to help, too."

"What? So they are both still in there?"

"I don't know."

Adam started shouting, "Eve! Logan! Can you hear me? Logan! Eve!"

"Shut up! I think I hear something," said Dominic.

It was faint but it was Logan. Dominic strained to pick out the words over the rush of the water, "Eve...legs...pull...."

"What's he saying?" asked Adam.

"Shh! I can't tell. I think he has Eve."

"Logan! Come toward us. There's a ledge to hold onto!" yelled Adam.

"...legs wedged...afraid..."

"I think they're stuck," said Dominic. "We may have to go in after them."

"How? We barely made it out."

"I know. But we don't have a choice. I would give anything for some rope."

"Okay," Adam sounded subdued. "If we're going we'd better go. They won't last long in that current."

Dominic groaned and stuck his legs back into the water. He felt along the side wall for the ledge to grip. Just as he was about to slide off the bank, something floppy struck him in the legs, tangling around his foot. Before he could stop himself, he yelled, imagining nasty water creatures living in the dark. But then he realized that it didn't have the texture of a fish. He reached down and pulled, using his hands to feel what his eyes couldn't see. It was long and thin, with knots every so often. Much thicker than rope, but it was some sort of cloth material, only wet and heavy.

"Hey, this is a sweatshirt!" Adam was beside him feeling the strange item. "Here's its hood."

Something clicked into place in Dominic's mind. Alex. She had made them a rope. Dominic's heart swelled with hope for the first time.

"Logan! Hold on! We have a rope! We're throwing it to you!"

"...rope?"

"Just hold on! When it gets to you, grab on and yell!"

Adam held one end of the rope while Dominic threw the other as far as he could out into the surging water.

"Did it reach you? Do you have it?"

"...can't see..."

"It didn't make it," Dominic said to Adam. "We need to pull it in and try over."

Frantically, they hauled in the makeshift rope and cast it out again. This time they heard a shout.

"Do you have it?"

"...touched...wait..."

They waited in tense silence for a moment.

"Got it!"

Practically crying with relief, Adam and Dominic both pulled on the rope and slowly, hand over hand, dragged Logan toward them. They couldn't see him, but they heard his *oof* of surprise when he hit the bank. On hands and knees, Dominic reached over and helped pull Logan up. He was clutching Eve with one hand and the rope with the other. Adam dragged Eve up onto the edge. She wasn't talking.

"Is she breathing?" asked Dominic.

Adam was huddled over her. "I can't tell." Dominic could hear the sounds of Adam starting CPR.

"She was talking when I first crashed into her, but then at some point she went under and I think she swallowed some water," said Logan.

Adam was counting softly to himself. Suddenly there was a gagging sound, and Adam jumped back, crashing into Dominic. "Eew. She puked on me."

"So sorry," said Eve through violent coughs.

And then they were all laughing, huddled together and unable to stop themselves. Dominic couldn't see the others, but just feeling them around him and knowing that somehow they had all survived was like a drug. After a few minutes, they finally calmed down.

"Where did you get that rope?" asked Logan.

"It floated down the river to us," Dominic said. "Alex must have made it. It feels like all our clothes tied together. What happened to you? How did you find Eve?"

"I crashed into her when I hit the wall. She grabbed on to me and we almost went through the outlet, but I managed to wedge my legs against the opening and hold on. At some point I felt her start to let go and realized that she had swallowed water. I tried to hold her above the water, but it was impossible to move without getting sucked through. If it hadn't been for that rope, we would have been goners."

The rope reminded Dominic. "Alex must be worried. We need to go back up stream and find her."

227

"How are we supposed to do that without any light?" asked Logan.

"Slowly, I guess," said Eve weakly.

They all laughed again, hysteria just barely kept at bay. "At least Alex should still have a light when we find her, not that I'll get much benefit from it," said Adam. "I lost my glasses in the water."

"Speaking of light," said Logan. "Do you guys see that?"

They did. Far away, a tiny point of light was moving toward them.

Chapter 19

What Light Flickers

Left alone on the bank of a rushing river in a giant underground cavern, sick with worry about her friends, and feeling the dark press in around her as if it would extinguish her little flashlight, it was easily the worst moment of Alex's life.

She saw Logan and Dominic dive into the water and disappear from sight, and a panic rose up in her throat, almost choking her. In that moment, it was all she could do to keep from throwing herself into the water as well. But Dominic's last words to her were still ringing in her ears. *Find something to use as a rope.* Her panic took a new direction.

She began to rummage, snatching up each backpack and dumping its contents on the ground. A few items caught her eye but were rejected nearly as quickly as they were seized upon. Some rubber bands. A necklace. Dental floss. At that last one, Alex screamed in frustration. This was useless. There was nothing. Then her eye fell on the ace bandage from her first aid kit. But, no, it was only about two feet long. Unless...

With sudden inspiration, Alex whirled around and seized the pile of discarded clothes. It was perfect. Starting with the socks, she tied everything together, carefully double and triple knotting, praying that getting wet would make the knot stronger. Unsure how long a rope would be needed, she stripped off her own socks and shoes, adding the laces to the very end. That was it. The best she could do.

Gathering up the whole hodgepodge pile in her hand and balancing her flashlight on top, she began to make her way downstream as quickly as possible. She had only gone about four feet when she slipped and, unable to catch her balance with her hands so full, sprawled face first on the rocky ground. The soft rope cushioned her fall, and she was unhurt, but her flashlight rolled off with a thunk and went out.

By this time she could hear yelling very faintly from up ahead. There was no time to lose. She felt frantically around for the flashlight with no luck. She knew she had no chance of feeling her way along in the dark. Another yell reached her. There was no choice.

Alex stood up and began slowly creeping along, praying she wouldn't misstep and fall into the water. Two steps, three, four. She tried unsuccessfully to remember how far away the end of the cavern was. More yelling. Five steps, six steps. She bashed her bare toe on a rock and cried out in pain. Seven steps, eight.

With no warning, her right foot came down in about a foot of water. She fell sideways this time, into the river. Flinging out her hands to catch herself, Alex let go of the rope. The water wasn't deep, and Alex was able to get back up on the bank in no time, but the rope was gone, carried away by the rapid water.

Alex collapsed in despair. She sat huddled alone on the bank in the dark, sobbing and dripping and shivering uncontrollably, listening as the shouting from downstream continued. She didn't know if she could bear to hear the last drowning cries of her friends. Alex covered her ears and cried harder. She had no idea how long she sat there, but at some point she heard something that caused her to raise her head. It was quiet.

Was that it then? Were they all dead?

A sudden sense of horror at being alone in the dark with all her dead friends spurred Alex into action. She crawled back upstream, feeling carefully around for her lost flashlight. When she arrived at the pile of junk that was the emptied out backpacks and realized that she had missed the flashlight, she had to stifle another sob. She turned back, this time walking and trying to count the steps she had taken before falling. A few steps in, she stepped on it, falling for the third time and skinning both knees. Clutching the precious plastic tube to her chest, she felt for the switch. A few frantic flips of the switch and a tightening of the battery cover later, the light came on. Alex cried out in hysterical relief.

Now that she had the light, she had to decide what to do. Should she just head out of the cave and go get help? Or should she attempt to look for her friends? Was there any chance that anyone was still alive? The thought of hunting by herself in the dark and maybe finding someone's body washed up on the bank was almost more than she could bear. But in the end, she knew she couldn't just leave without knowing for sure that no one still needed her help. With only a short pause to put her shoes back on, Alex headed downstream again.

Now that she had the light to guide her and her shoes to protect her feet, it didn't really take that long before she could see the wall of the cavern looming up ahead of her. The roaring sound of the river was getting louder as she approached the place where the water crashed against the rock face, but she began to imagine that she could hear something else over the rushing sound. Was that laughter?

Heart pounding, Alex moved forward even quicker. Suddenly she heard shouting from the other side of the river. She couldn't make out all the words, but she definitely heard her own name.

"I'm here!" she yelled. "Are you okay?" Alex leaned forward with her flashlight, but the river was just too wide.

There was some response, but she couldn't understand it.

"I can't hear you!"

More indistinguishable shouting followed this and then a pause. Finally several voices in unison reached her, "Go upstream!"

Alex did, moving slowly, aware that the others would be walking without the aid of a flashlight. From time to time she shined her light out across the water. Even though she couldn't see the other side, she hoped they could see her light and that maybe it would help them walk.

When she arrived back at the pile of discarded belongings, Alex stopped to wait, leaving her light trained on the river. It was several minutes before she heard the yelling again. The water was a little quieter here, and this time she could hear Dominic's voice, faint but clear.

"We're all okay. We made it."

The relief was so overwhelming that Alex started to tremble again. Her legs gave way beneath her and she sank down on the pile of shoes.

"Are you okay?" This time it was Adam's voice.

It took a couple of tries for Alex to summon enough strength for her voice to be heard. "I'm fine."

"What now?" came the call from a across the water.

Good question, thought Alex, what now? Either they all had to get back across the water, or she had to cross to them. If they were to go on, she would need to cross. But how? And how would they get home when they had finished? She sat for quite a while thinking, but she knew all along what she was going to say.

"Let's get me across."

There was some muffled shouting before Dominic's voice said, "If you wade out half way we can throw you the rope before you get to the drop off."

"Okay."

"Bring shoes!" yelled Eve.

Alex nodded to herself. She gathered up all the shoes and the first aid kit, now mostly empty, and stuffed them into one pack. As an afterthought, she grabbed an empty backpack for carrying back the books, if they found them.

"Have a little faith," she muttered to herself. Surely it wasn't possible to go through all this for nothing.

She was already ankle deep in the water when Adam's voice reached her again. "Bring the sword."

Alex looked around. The sword was lying off to the side where she hadn't even noticed it before. She snatched it up, wondering how she was going swim and hold a rope and the sword at the same time.

It didn't end up being that hard. Halfway across the river, she could make out the shapes of her four friends on the far bank. If Alex thought hearing their voices was wonderful, it couldn't even compare to the relief of seeing them in front of her. Dominic and Logan were holding the rope between them, and when she stopped, they threw it together. Alex was able to grab it in one hand on the first try. At Dominic's instruction, she wrapped the end several times around her hand and then began to walk again. After a few steps, her footing disappeared and Alex felt a momentary panic, but then the rope pulled taut in her hand and she started to kick in the direction it was pulling. In a matter of moments, hands were reaching out to haul her up on the bank and her friends were all around her. In the pale light of the single flashlight, she could see them all, beaming even while they shivered and interrupting each other in their haste to hear and tell everyone's part of the story.

Alex was cold. She was wet and tired and still shaking with the shock of the last hour. But she couldn't remember ever being so happy.

Chapter 20

The Stolen Toy, The Father's Love

There was only one tunnel on this side of the river, and it was narrow enough to force them to walk single file again. Adam, the last in the line, was thankful for the tight quarters because it gave him an excuse not to have to face the others.

Everyone had asked and answered all their questions without anyone bringing up Adam's stupidity in going into the water in the first place. Still, Adam knew sooner or later he needed to admit what an idiot he had been. He felt a lump in the pit of his stomach at the thought of what might have happened. It was nothing short of a miracle that no one had drowned. And he knew it was all his fault.

There was no way around it. The more he thought about it, the more sick and ashamed he felt. He had insisted on going into the water without a rope even though he knew it was the dumbest thing imaginable. He had been too impatient. Worse, he hadn't wanted to listen to Dominic's advice because he was jealous of Dominic. Now that he was forcing himself to be honest, Adam knew that he had intentionally disagreed with everything Dominic said because he felt like they were competing for the leadership of the group. Stupid? Yes. But there it was. He was jealous of Dominic because the others listened to him. When they had first begun, Adam was the unofficial leader, but all that changed when Dominic came along.

So now I'm so petty that I would rather risk everyone's lives than listen to Dominic's good advice? Adam was disgusted by himself. He knew this was no time for apologies, but he silently promised that he would take responsibility as soon as they were out of this cave. He hoped that he would have some chance to make it up to the others.

He was so taken up with these thoughts that he crashed into Logan before he realized that everyone had stopped in front of him.

"What's going on?" Adam couldn't see anything past Logan's head.

"I think we're here," whispered Alex from the front of the line.

238

"It's another cavern," said Dominic softly. "And this one is full."

Slowly they all stepped forward until they were standing side by side in the new cavern. Alex's flashlight played over a massive mound of mauled books and miscellaneous junk. Even without the aid of his glasses, Adam could see that almost all the books were torn, burned, and shredded within an inch of their lives. Loose pages were everywhere.

It was beyond comprehension. Whatever Adam was expecting to find at the end of their journey, it sure wasn't this. There must have been thousands of books, all apparently destroyed. Who could have done this?

No sooner had Adam thought the question than Eve voiced it.

"No way it was just one person," said Dominic.

"Someone really hates books," Alex said.

"Or just one book," suggested Logan.

The reminder of what they were here to find turned Adam's stomach. Were their books in this pile? Had they met the same fate as all these others? His heart sank at the thought that their efforts had been for nothing.

"Do you think our books are here?" Eve voiced his thoughts again.

"Seems likely," said Adam. "The question is, are they in one piece?"

"Seems unlikely," said Eve.

"Well, we'd better look," Dominic said.

"There's no point in spreading out," said Alex. "We only have one light. But I'll try to hold it up, so you can all look around a bit."

"I think I'm glad we can't split up," said Eve. "It creeps me out to think of whoever did this coming back to find us."

"Good point," said Dominic. "We don't know if the thief is here or not."

"Just sitting in the dark?" asked Adam, then silently cursed himself for using that snarky tone again. Was he incapable of normal conversation?

"I don't know," Dominic said. "I'm just saying keep your eyes open."

"Anyway, we know it's probably not human," said Logan. "Maybe it doesn't need light."

With that encouraging thought, they all moved to the pile and began sorting through the rubble to find any books that might still be whole.

"Here's something," said Eve. "It has a red cover...I think it's a Book of Sight! It is! The cover
240

is pretty scorched, but it doesn't look like any pages have fallen out."

Logan looked at it. "Yes, it definitely is."

Hope filled Adam. Maybe they would be able to find, or at least replace, all of their books after all. With renewed energy, they all began searching again.

"What's that?" asked Alex, pointing from where she held the light a little ways distant to maximize the beam.

Dominic went to check it out. "It's another one," he called excitedly.

"I think I've got one here, too," said Adam. He stuck it along with the others in the empty backpack Alex had brought.

For a while it was quiet as they searched. Any time someone saw even a part of the Book of Sight that was recognizable, they put it in the bag.

"I found something," said Logan. "It's a book, but it's not the same. Someone wrote in it, like a journal or something."

He held up the tattered remains of a book which may once have been a journal with a green cover but now looked as if it had been set on fire and then soaked in water and then trampled by a herd of elephants. Adam doubted it would be of much help, but he reached out for it just the same.

Before Logan could hand it over, however, several things happened very fast. Eve screamed, a shadow passed in front of Adam knocking Logan to the floor, and Alex cried out in pain and dropped the flashlight. With a terrifying *thunk* the flashlight landed on the cavern floor and everything went dark.

Chapter 21

Hand in Hand
and Back to Back

Head throbbing, Logan woke up to blackness and chaos. For one completely disoriented moment, he couldn't remember anything.

Then out of the chaos of sounds around him, one voice broke through his mental haze.

"Alex! You guys, help me!"

Logan leapt to his feet, was overtaken by vertigo, overcorrected, and stumbled to his knees again. Apparently quick movement wasn't happening for him. But at least now he could remember where he was and what had happened. He hadn't seen whatever hit him, but it had been moving fast and when he fell, he must have hit his head on a rock.

Before his head could stop spinning, something else crashed into him and he found himself struggling for air at the bottom of a pile of writhing arms and legs and...something else. Something smooth and supple and strong.

Terrifying images leapt to life in Logan's head. Giant snakes and nameless but fearsome amphibious creatures. He imagined a flat nose perfectly designed for smelling its prey and powerful muscles for squeezing and delicate fangs dripping venom.

Overcome with horror, he kicked out violently, clawing for a way to escape, receiving blows on all sides from unseen sources. He could hear grunting and a cry of pain. Someone's elbow hit him in the stomach and all breath was knocked from his body at the same ghastly moment that his hands glanced off not one but two thick rubbery snakes.

Logan thought he could never have imagined a situation more horrible than this one, fighting something vile that he couldn't even see. He was only a fraction away from utter mindless panic when he was suddenly blinded by a light.

The shock was enough to clear his head instantly and he had just a moment to register the complete blackness of the creature next to his face before it shuddered in one giant muscle spasm and threw him off, along with Adam and Dominic, who had been clutching its arms.

But they weren't arms. They were tentacles. The creature was like some kind of land-crawling octopus, so black that it defied the light. It wasn't particularly large, but the gruesomely bulbous head resting on its powerful tentacles was terrifying. If it had a mouth, Logan didn't see it. All his revulsion was focused on the two enormous bulging eyes, dark and unblinking. Could this really be the thief that had entered his trailer at night? He shuddered at the thought, but all doubt was erased as it turned noiselessly and ran with incredible eight-legged speed toward Eve, who stood in shock, holding the flashlight Alex had dropped.

Logan barely had time to notice Alex, apparently just released, gasping for breath next to him. Then the creature hit Eve at full speed and she crumpled to the ground, the flashlight, miraculously still lit, rolling far out of reach. In the dim light, Logan could see the black form (black, so black) wrapping itself around Eve, slowly crushing her.

No venomous fangs here but still an unspeakable menace. He hurled himself at the monster, Adam and Dominic alongside him, grasping for a hold on the smooth, strong tentacles.

"The sword, Adam, the sword!" yelled Dominic.

Adam fumbled for his sword, raised it high and brought it down swiftly on the tentacle in front of him. There was a hideous *thwap*, and the sword bounced off, dropping uselessly to the ground as Adam collapsed with a scream, clutching his right arm in agony.

Dominic yelled in rage and began pummeling, but it seemed to feel his blows even less than the sword. Logan could see Eve's face turning purple. An awful sort of desperation filled his heart, even more blinding than the panic which had seized him in the dark. He reached out, feeling the unyielding rubber beneath his hands, and jammed his fingers into what may have been the thing's nose. It snapped its head so hard it almost broke his wrist but didn't release its hold on Eve.

"That's it!" Dominic cried and flung his hands into the creature's eye.

The beast, which until now had been completely silent, let out a low bellow that seemed to come from underneath its body and turned with that awe-inspiring speed, dropping Eve as it focused on Dominic. Before Logan had even realized what had happened, Dominic was wrapped tight. He clearly couldn't breath, but he managed to whisper the word, "Eyes."

Logan saw exactly what he had to do. Praying that he wouldn't accidently hit Dominic, Logan snatched up Adam's sword and aimed it at the black eye. A quick breath, and he plunged it in.

This time the bellow was almost deafening. Something about the sound drained all the adrenalin from Logan's body. He was overcome with the awful ugliness of what he had just done. He thought he might be sick right then and there.

But it was done. The creature had released Dominic and was thrashing around on the ground, inky blood streaming from its wound. Writhing and convulsing, it backed away from where they all were grouped, its bellows fading slowly into gurgles. It stopped a short way away, shuddering and shaking. It seemed to be gathering its strength for one final attack. Logan saw Dominic pulling himself over to where the sword was lying.

Whatever he was planning was unnecessary. With a tremendous heave, their enemy lifted a tentacle and brought it down with a shattering crunch. Its final act had been to crush the flashlight, leaving them all in blackness once more.

Chapter 22

The Song is Renewed

Alex was remembering something her dad always used to say when he took her camping. Walking in the dark is often easier when you have no light at all. A little light just makes the darkness all around seem like an enemy, but without light, you are forced to make your peace with the dark, and it can even be a friend.

Alex thought she might have some arguments with that theory. She'd been trying pretty hard to make her peace with this dark, but shuffling slowly through a small passageway without any help from her eyes or any way to see how far they still had to go was not something she found very friendly.

They had started the return journey as soon as Eve and Dominic had fully regained their breath. No one had wanted to wait in the pitch black cavern with a dead monster only a few yards away. An *apparently* dead monster. They already had a few copies of the book in the backpack, so they grabbed hands and felt their way to the exit passage as quickly as possible.

No one was talking much, and Alex wondered if, like her, they were all thinking about the cold, dark river to be crossed ahead. She hoped her hand on Eve's shoulder ahead of her felt as reassuring as Dominic's hand on her own shoulder. You might not be able to see me, that hand said, but I'm right here with you. In light of all they had just accomplished together, that was a very good feeling.

Because they had done it. Even with the dark all around and the obstacles ahead, Alex felt a sense of triumph slowly growing in her heart. They had won. They had survived all the dangers. They had defeated the black thief. They had found their stolen books.

Just the thought of the book made the triumphant feeling grow.

"Gendel sea," she whispered to herself.

Dominic squeezed her shoulder.

Fortunately, crossing the river again wasn't very difficult. Cold and wet, but not difficult. Alex had worried that they might not be able to find their rope in the dark, but they stumbled on it almost immediately.

250

Adam volunteered to swim across first, with the rope clutched tightly in his hand, of course. Alex held her breath as they waited, sightless, for him to call out that he had found sure footing. Soon he did, and it was only a matter of moments after that before they were all struggling through the shallow water and up the far bank, Logan coming last and holding the backpack of books above his head.

The trip through the second tunnel was much better than the first, partially because the obstacle of the river was past and partially because halfway through there began to be a little light ahead. Alex had never loved the light as much as she did now. She thought of a few things she would like to say to her dad about his theories on darkness.

As soon as they saw the light, everyone started moving faster. By the end, they were tripping over each other as they burst, laughing and blinking, into the warm sunshine.

The next thing Alex knew, she was being tightly hugged by Eve. Then Adam and Logan and even Dominic were all joining in, piled together in a big group. As her eyes finally adjusted, Alex saw tears on Eve's face, though she was smiling.

"I can't believe we made it," she said. "We actually made it."

They broke apart and sank to the ground on the dry pebbles of the creek bed. Logan stretched out, his face turned to the sun in bliss. Dominic was examining the cuts on his arm. Eve began to open the backpack, but Adam cut in.

"Before we get the books out, there's really something I should say." He paused, not looking at anyone. "I'm sorry. I totally put you all in danger back there at the river. I was stupid and impatient and...well, I wanted to prove something. I'm sorry. I could have gotten someone killed."

For a minute no one said anything. Alex wondered what the right thing would be to say. She didn't hold anything against Adam, but she wished that she could be like Logan and know just by looking at Adam what he needed to hear. She was a little surprised when it was Eve who spoke up.

"We're all stupid sometimes, Adam. Forget about it. I'd trust you with my life anytime."

Alex could see the tears in Adam's eyes, just before he turned away. "Thanks," he said in a low voice.

"Now let's check these out," said Eve. She turned over the backpack, and four beat up books and several torn covers and loose pages fell out.

Alex was just starting to open hers, when Eve said, "Hey! Look at this, guys!"

She was holding up the remains of the green book that Logan had found. Most of the pages were illegible, either from burn marks or water smudges. Still, they all huddled around while Eve carefully flipped through it. Finally she found something that caught all of their attention.

"...can't see...don't want anyone to read...so beautiful...would want to hide the book..."

"This is it," said Adam excitedly. "Someone else who has read the book!"

But nothing else on that page or the next several pages was legible. Finally, just three pages from the end, Eve found a paragraph that was almost intact.

"We succeeded in destroying Stafa's lair, but the shadow stalker himself was not there. We found very few books still in a condition to be reclaimed, but those we have we will guard carefully. The other treasures were brought into the light. He will not be returning there. There is little doubt that he will find a new lair soon. We must be on the lookout. ...hinting that there are many about even more dangerous than the pilpi, but when we question them, they just give you that mysterious smile. Sometimes I wonder whose side they're on. Of course, to know that, I'd have to know whose side *we're* on. Still, there's something about them I don't quite trust. That feeling is getting pretty common these days.

But I know what I do trust. I trust the book. And I trust the other readers. All but…"

"That's it," said Eve, examining the last few pages. "All the rest is completely stained."

"Not much to go on," said Alex.

"But more than we had before," Adam said. "I think we can safely say that creature we just killed was named Stafa."

"What was that about 'many about even more dangerous'?" asked Eve.

"That sounds like a problem for another day," said Dominic.

"I just wish we could have found something that told us what this was all about, you know?" said Adam.

Eve was still absently flipping through the pages, frowning at the smudged writing.

"What was that?" asked Logan.

A little slip of paper had drifted down from the journal and landed at Alex's feet. She picked it up, read it, and held it silently up to the others. It was written in the same hand as the journal.

If anyone out there is reading this, know that you are not alone. Concerning the Book of Sight, we have very few answers. But we believe that we have finally discovered the true

questions. Not 'where did it come from?'
Not 'why were we chosen?' But rather,
'what are we meant to do now?' And
'who is it that will stand in our way?'

Afterword

In a plain house on a dull street in a nondescript neighborhood in a sleepy town near the mountains lived a girl named Alex. She was, as far as most people could tell, a perfectly average teenage girl. Average grades, average talents, average pastimes, average friends.

But there were those who knew the truth.

More importantly, Alex herself knew the truth, and that was what enabled her to get up on ordinary mornings like this and lead her ordinary life with that kind of inner happiness that people like to call joy.

On this morning, the last lazy morning of summer vacation, she woke up early, hoping to reduce her mountain of laundry to a hill before lunchtime. She was absorbed in doing just that (with a heavy red book lying open on the top of the dryer) when her father stuck his head into the laundry room.

"Hard at work again, Magna?"

"Dad! I wasn't expecting to see you today. Just getting some laundry done for school tomorrow."

"Oh wow, that's tomorrow already? I thought you still had another week. I guess I really have been out of it lately, huh?"

"No more than usual," Alex smiled. "Does this surprise visit mean that you've finished?"

"Unfortunately, no. I have a long way to go yet, but even I can't ignore the call of nature forever."

Alex laughed.

"So is there anything you still need? Should we go back-to-school shopping today?"

"Nope. I took care of it. You gave me that money last Friday, remember?"

"I gave you money? I don't remember that at all." He raised his eyebrows in mock horror. "I'm even more dangerous than I thought. I certainly hope you don't take advantage of me in my vulnerable state."

"You'll never know, will you?"

"So what else have I been missing out on?" he asked, only half-joking.

Alex took a long time to answer. "Quite a bit, actually, but it's kind of a long story."

Before she could say more, the doorbell rang. Alex stood looking at her dad for a moment.

"I'd better get that," she said finally.

"Okay," he said. "But I'll take a rain check on that long story."

"Deal."

He had already disappeared back into his studio by the time Alex opened the front door. On the porch stood her friend Dominic. His face was only slightly less impassive than usual.

"Hey, Dom, what's up?"

"I just got a letter back from my mom," he said in his usual direct way. "We're all meeting at the Redoubt as soon as we can. I thought I'd see if you wanted to walk with me if you're free."

"Sure," said Alex. "Just let me get my book. I can't believe she wrote back so soon."

"Yeah," said Dominic. "And Alex, you aren't going to believe what she said."

Turn the page for a
sneak peak of

The Broken Circle

Book 2
Of
The Book of Sight

Now available for sale
in paperback and e-book.

His hair whipped into a frenzy by the gusting wind, Dominic stood staring into the smoking pit. A hole the size of a house was surrounded by piles of dirt and twisted tree limbs. The thick smoke made it impossible to see how deep it went. What twenty minutes ago had been an overgrown creek bank was now a crater. If Dominic hadn't been passing nearby on his bike when he felt the force of the blast and saw the earth flying through the sky, he wouldn't have believed such a thing possible.

"Hey kid, get back from there! You shouldn't be anywhere near here."

The voice and the heavy hand on his shoulder jolted Dominic back into the real world. He turned to look up into the face of the firefighter.

"This area is off limits. Still very dangerous. You need to get back. We're roping off the whole site." When Dominic still didn't respond, the man's face softened a bit. "Are you okay, kid? Were you hurt in the explosion?"

Dominic shook his head and allowed himself to be led back toward the jumble of flashing lights that represented every emergency vehicle the city of Dunmore owned. Men and women with serious faces and official uniforms swarmed everywhere.

Slowly Dominic's head cleared. The fireman who was gripping his arm had brought him to the nearest ambulance.

Dominic pulled away. "I'm not hurt."

The fireman looked at him closely. "Your arm is cut, and you look pretty shaken up, kid. How close were you when the explosion happened?"

"Not that close. I was on the road...on my bike. When it blew up, my bike tipped over. But it's no big deal. I'm okay. Sorry I went over there. I just wanted to see what happened."

"Curiosity is natural, kid. No one's going to put you in jail for that. Let the guys clean your arm up and then you get on home. But you stay away from here from now on, you hear? This site's going to be dangerous for quite a while, and until we've figured out what caused the blast, no one is allowed anywhere near. This is no game, kid. You understand?"

"Yes, sir."

"All right then. Joey here can take care of you."

Dominic was silent while the EMT disinfected and bandaged the scrape on his arm. When it was finished, he said a polite thank you and went to get his bike. It was still lying where he had left it by the side of the road.

It wasn't until he was pedaling home that he allowed himself to think about what this meant.

That explosion site was the same place where last summer he and his friends had discovered a cave that was home to a dangerous, thieving monster, called a pilpi. The pilpi had stolen something valuable from them, and when they had gone to get it back, it had attacked them, forcing them to kill it in order to escape. Of course, no one else in town knew about that. No one else in town would even believe there was such a creature as a pilpi. That was because no one else in town had ever read the Book of Sight.

The previous summer, some of Dominic's friends had received a mysterious old book, delivered to their front doors. After they read it, they began to see things that had always been around them but they had never noticed before. Dominic hadn't gotten a book himself. He still wondered about that sometimes, worried that whoever sent the books hadn't thought that he deserved one. He had been left to find things out because of an old painting in his grandparents' house.

Anyway, he had read the book now. He had his own copy, pieced together from pages rescued from the pilpi's hoard. What's more, now he knew that he wasn't the first person in his family to have one. He remembered how excited he had been when his mother's letter arrived from Mexico.

I can't believe you got a hold of a Book. I did not think there were any left for you to find. If your abuela told you that the painting was mine, then you will already have guessed the truth. I had a Book once, and so did your father. The painting was given to us by someone in our circle. I should have burned it long ago, but your abuela begged to keep it, and I never thought it could do harm hanging in the back hall of my mother's house.

Dominic's excitement had faded into disbelief at the bitterness that bled through every line.

I don't want to remember those days. In time, that Book took away everything I loved, and if that isn't enough to convince you to destroy it, there is nothing more I can say.

There may have been nothing more to say, but she kept writing him just the same. Every few weeks another letter would come, full of the same dark hints and warnings. She never answered any of his questions, just repeated over and over that horrible things would be coming.

It nagged at him now. Not the extraordinary fact that someone...or something...had blown up the pilpi's cave. Not the obvious questions as to who would want to do that...and why. Dominic couldn't stop thinking about something his mother had said in her last letter, something that made him wonder if she knew this was going to happen.

Dominic was so preoccupied with this last thought that he sped right past his grandfather rocking on the front porch and would have headed straight upstairs to his room if his grandmother hadn't stopped him with a firm grasp of his arm.

"Dominico, me alegro verte. Sentimos los temblores y nos preocupamos. Estás bien?"

Was he okay? Dominic wasn't totally sure, but he nodded his head anyway. He felt a little surge of guilt that he hadn't even thought that his grandmother might worry.

Now she was fixing him with that laser stare that always seemed to know too much. She didn't ask many questions, but Dominic was pretty sure that was because she didn't have to. She could just read his mind instead.

"I'm fine, Abue. There was an explosion. My bike tipped over, but I didn't get hurt." He didn't mention where the explosion was. Though they knew about the Book of Sight, he had never told his grandparents about the pilpi's cave and what happened there. He didn't want to worry them. His grandmother had enough worries these days with his grandfather's health.

His abuela continued to hold his eyes, but he just looked back as calmly as he could, trying to push down his desperation to get upstairs to his room. After a minute she nodded and turned back to her stove, only saying that dinner would be ready in half an hour.

Dominic took the stairs two at a time.

In his room he reached under the bed for the box that contained all of his mother's letters. He rifled through them to find the one he wanted and skimmed through it for the words he remembered.

...I know you think this is a grand adventure, mijo, but you do not understand what will face you, powers that are greater than you can imagine, powers that can call down water from the sky and fire from the earth...

Fire from the earth. Was that what had happened today? Had some unseen power caused that explosion? Dominic wished he could ask his mother these questions. She obviously knew something about it. Just as obviously, she didn't want him to know.

...I will not say more. I have told you before, this is not a case in which knowledge makes you safer. Knowing things will only put you in more danger. Please, mijo, whatever you already know, try to forget it.

Dominic frowned, filled with the same anger her letters always caused. He wasn't a child. He didn't need her to protect him. And how could she think he would ever forget what he had learned from the Book of Sight?

He had seen messages in the sky that had saved his life. He had seen a tree stump talking. He had seen leaves glow and transform into jewels right before his eyes. And he had met friends who already knew him better than his mother ever had.

Whatever danger there might be, he would never trade what he had found because he was afraid. There was no going back. His mother should know that. She had obviously read the book herself. What could have happened to make her write the way she did now?

Dominic crumpled the paper in one fist. He would never know what had happened because she would not tell him. He tossed the letter on the bed, not willing to even look at the last bit she had written.

...As for these new friends, you say that you trust them completely. Be careful, mijo. You can never count on what anyone will do when you really need them.

About the Author

Deborah Dunlevy was born in Indiana and grew up everywhere else. Even moving every year or two couldn't satisfy her desire for adventure, so she learned how to read and started taking trips into other people's lives. Eventually she grew up and went to college and got a respectable job as a teacher. Then she ditched that to go live on the other side of the world, where she had a few kids and learned what adventure was really about.

Deborah now lives in Indianapolis with her husband, Nate, her three kids, and an Argentine hound dog. She spends her time making up stories and sometimes writing them down on her blog tellmeastorymommy.com.

Made in the USA
San Bernardino, CA
31 August 2013